TEMP

Nikki stared at him with... said, "I don't want you. Far from letting you make love to me, I wouldn't even let you touch me."

He stood frowning, his eyes wild.

"On the other hand," she said, "I *will* let you touch me." She pointed to the ottoman. "Sit down."

Penstone nodded dumbly, sat, and looked at her.

"You may touch my foot," she said calmly, "with your lips."

She extended her foot. He cupped it in his palm and kissed her arch.

She sat with her arms folded, grinning at him contemptuously. He turned so red his face looked ready to burst. Suddenly he leaped up to seize her ankles, pulling her toward him . . .

AUTHOR'S PROFILE

Recognized as one of America's outstanding contemporary novelists, Stuart Friedman began his writing career in 1938 after first trying his luck in the advertising field, working as a real estate agent and heading up the operation of a labor-industry counseling service.

Born in the Midwest, Mr. Friedman devoted his first writing efforts to the publication of a comprehensive history on the State of Indiana. Since that first venture, he has written more than a dozen novels.

One of Monarch Books' top selling authors with sales of more than 2 million copies overall, he is, perhaps, best known for his current favorites: THE SURGEONS, IRINA and FATHERS AND DAUGHTERS.

CURRENT BESTSELLING MONARCH BOOKS

MS21	THE COOL BOOK by Art Unger	50¢
MS19	THEY FOUGHT UNDER THE SEA by The Editors of Navy Times	50¢
MS18	WHAT'S WRONG WITH U.S. FOREIGN POLICY? by Frank L. Kluckhohn	75¢
MS17	SKIN AND SCUBA DIVING by Richard Hardwick	50¢
MS16	THE CRISIS IN CUBA by Thomas Freeman	50¢
MS13	HOW TO STAY YOUNG AND BEAUTIFUL by Jan Michael	50¢
MS11	THE RED CARPET by Ezra Taft Benson	75¢
MS8	THE COLD WAR by Deane and David Heller	50¢
MS6	THE NAKED RISE OF COMMUNISM by Frank L. Kluckhohn	75¢
MS3B	AMERICA: LISTEN! by Frank L. Kluckhohn	95¢

(Second new enlarged edition. Completely updated.) An honest report to the nation on the current chaos in Washington.

K70	THE ANATOMY OF RAPE by Gary Gordon	50¢
MB539	THE GIRL MARKET by Ann Marie and Michael Burgess	50¢
MB538	YOU AND YOUR SEX LIFE by L. T. Woodward, M.D.	50¢
MB536	CANCER AND YOU by Martin James, M.D.	50¢
MB535	THE SEXUALLY PROMISCUOUS FEMALE by Benjamin Morse, M.D.	50¢
MB534	GIRLS AND GANGS by Don James	50¢
MB533	THE IMPOTENT MALE by Dr. Leland E. Glover	50¢
MB532	PROSTITUTION AROUND THE WORLD by Stan Burnett and Alan Seeger	60¢
MA350	THE U.S. NAVY IN ACTION by John Clagett	75¢
MA319	U.S. MARINES IN ACTION by T. R. Fehrenbach	50¢
380	SEASON FOR LOVE by Whitman Chambers	40¢
372	THE GANG GIRLS by Carson Bingham	40¢
370	THE CHILLINGWORTH MURDER CASE by Ernie Hutter	50¢
364	WILD TO POSSESS by Gil Brewer	40¢

Available at all newsstands and bookstores

If you are unable to secure these books at your local dealer, you may obtain copies by sending the retail price plus 5¢ for handling each title to Monarch Books, Inc., Mail Order Department, Division Street, Derby, Connecticut.

KEY BS-4

A Contemporary Novel

NIKKI REVISITED

Stuart Friedman

Author of FATHERS AND DAUGHTERS

MONARCH BOOKS, INC.

Derby, Connecticut

NIKKI REVISITED

A Monarch Books Original Novel

Published in October, 1963

Copyright © 1963 by Stuart Friedman

And yet again . . .
        to the best of them. . . .
                Jeanette Arnold Friedman

Cover Painting by Tom Miller

Monarch Books are published by MONARCH BOOKS, INC., Capital Building, Derby, Connecticut, and represent the works of outstanding novelists and writers of non-fiction especially chosen for their literary merit and reading entertainment.

Printed in the United States of America

All Rights Reserved

Chapter One

The air was perfumed by seventy acres of white-blossoming apple trees when Nikki, vividly beautiful with her red hair dazzling in the sunlight, drove up in a low, powerful, white sports car. The predominantly male crowd of earthy Virginians assembled there in her orchard that spring morning watched her with amiable lechery.

"Here's the queen bee herself," one of them drawled.

Another joked: "Nikki, with that hair of yours it's a good thing the honeybees are blind to the red end of the spectrum."

"Too bad men aren't," she said, grinning. "Too bad for them."

Those near the car laughed appreciatively. Gentlemen all, Nikki thought amusedly, they didn't seem to be waiting to look up her skirt while she was getting out of the car. It was almost unsporting of her to be so swiftly expert about the maneuver. Before they knew the game was over she was out and on the move; rumors that she always wore black lace panties or red lace or never wore any panties at all remained unconfirmed.

They opened a pathway for her as she went toward the bee truck, moving with a dancer's graceful rhythmic flow of balanced tensions. The custom fit of her sleeveless white blouse, full-swinging dark-green knee-length skirt and narrow red-leather Italian barefoot sandals defined the sleek elegance of her superb body. She carried herself proudly, her fine head lifted and slightly tilted to one side. Her face, with its high cheekbones, intense green eyes and alluring, though faintly mocking lips, glowed stunningly.

Satisfying her whole being was the tone of restless vitality and challenge that had made Nikki the college "Storm Front," then the fiercely competitive sports champion, glamorous international playgirl and darling of gossip columnists and photographers. That glittering aura of excitement had helped build her public image as an irresistible *femme fatale* who discarded suitors more casually than she did her Parisian gowns. The image had advantages, she knew, though it was generally false.

Nikki's fiery reality was spectacular enough. She subjected would-be lovers to tests from which they were likely to slink away, beaten. Not because she was frivolous. Far from it, she required qualities of character that she could respect in any man she allowed to become important in her life. If he lacked them, or the strength to master her, and submitted to her will, he wasn't man enough for Nikki Duquesne.

Her nearest neighbor, George Penstone, a big, coarse red-neck in his mid-thirties, who lusted for her sexy body, definitely wasn't man enough. With patient scorn Nikki had for months been forcing him to swallow that truth, bitter dose by bitter dose. It gagged him. Arrogantly male, he was contemptuous of women, and to be not only sexually frustrated by one but bested in other fields infuriated him. But he wouldn't learn not to tangle with her.

Their clash had begun last season. Nikki had realized in San Francisco that, since the shocking occasion of her parents' double funeral, her life had been purposeless flight. The guilts and fears connected with home had vanished and she'd returned. The beautiful, rolling land had been in her family a century and a half; and when she was a child the Duquesne estate had been a showplace.

But during her father's last years, when Nikki ruled him because he was fighting a hidden battle against incest with the help of too much booze, his spirit broke and the property declined. She, too, had neglected it and the dying look of its fields, barns, fences, roadways and once-magnificent main house had pierced her with a kind of anguish and shame.

She was determined to restore it to its rightful role as the finest in the area. But the enormous cost would force her to borrow heavily. Money aside, the project was immense, the responsibility for managing it a serious matter. She had the brains and ability, Nikki knew without a trace of false modesty, but she wasn't certain she had the temperament for the job.

The heaviness of the big empty house depressed her that first week. Standing in candlelight one night in the third-floor rooms she'd lived in as a girl, Nikki ached for that long-ago feel of her father's commanding, protective presence. She felt dreadfully alone and inadequate and wished she were weak and that she had someone to lean on and love and trust, someone who could make vital decisions for her. And there was no one. Because, she lashed herself, she was unworthy, a destroying savage who brought out the *worst* in everyone. Her touch would not bring back the lost beauty but blight the very soil. So, she thought with rising emotion, let this land and house which were her identity continue to rot like a public proclamation of her inner truth.

Or better, she thought, lowering her head, her shoulders drooping, she would accept that insulting price George Penstone had offered. He was big enough to salvage the property. She would go away, somewhere, not forsaking her home but driven from it. She would not have to see him striding the Duquesne land as its master, for she would never view it again. She felt tears forming hotly in the corners of her eyes and she pressed a fist to her breast as if her heart were breaking.

And then she thought: *The real tragedy, Nikki dear, is that there is no audience for this scene you are playing to the hilt. You know damned well you've made up your mind to put this place on its feet even if it does mean going for broke.*

Penstone's insulting offer was made through her lawyer in a written proposition. As the expiration date approached, she ignored it. She busied herself interviewing prospective foremen, hiring work crews, pricing machinery, equipment, materials, consulting contractors, suppliers, feed and seed dealers, livestock buyers, checking dates and locations of horse auctions.

There were 2,000 acres, 1,700 productive after deducting building areas and paddocks, access roads, creekland and woods. She drove through or tramped over most of it. She made notes, computing acres-per-head to determine the size of her proposed beef and dairy herds, calculated silo and bin space and stall-unit cost of new barns for thoroughbred race horse brood mares and stallions. Planning crops from apples to zucchini with off-season specialties from her four acres of greenhouses (requiring an acre of new glass) and including various hays for all seasons, corn, oats, soybeans, wheat or rye, she was confronted with hundreds of details.

On the go, physically or mentally, eighteen hours a day, the challenge stimulated her to a sense of exultant aliveness. Her rushing tempo made her impatient with problems. She thought of them as similar to tennis balls sizzling at her during a match point in a tournament finals, to be solved smashingly with split-second decisions.

She learned grudgingly but swiftly that she was not playing for trophies or matching skills and courage for victory thrills or gallery applause. Her whole life was in this game. She could lose it by snap judgments and though she made a few when the temptation to dramatize overwhelmed her, she usually resisted.

The discipline she imposed on herself gave her a sense of worth she hadn't had in years. At night she would drop into her bed tired with the good tiredness of having used herself fully and meaningfully. There would be an almost voluptuous feeling in her flesh, slow and sweet and warm as she closed her eyes and slept.

No time at all would seem to pass before she was up at dawn, sparkling with vitality, her alert green eyes wide-open and shining, a high-spirited, mischievous grin beginning to spread over her stunning face. She'd dash toward the shower, her sleek white body naked, red hair stirring loosely around her delicately sloping shoulders, her pertly uptilted dark-nippled young breasts bobbing prettily, her lovely legs lifting quickly, while her high, smooth bottom dimpled and rounded alternately in a lively rhythm.

Preparing to enter the shower on one such morning, she thought about Penstone with abrupt anger. A passionate, stormy expression intensified the beauty of her face and her eyes flashed with defiance. She'd calmly parried his first attempt to buy her out, telling him to add a zero to the last figure of his price. When he raised his bid a paltry few thousand, she made it clear that she didn't intend to sell. The thriving activity on her property made her intentions even clearer. But he had dared make another low bid, only yesterday.

He'd waylaid her in the town square and made the offer in his loud voice in front of several people. She stood, slight and sleek-lined as a thoroughbred racing filly against his strong, clumsy bulk, and heard him out. He spoke laughingly of the work she was doing on her place as if it were just a big show calculated to force his price up. And, he chuckled, she'd got her way: he was adding five thousand to his last offer.

When he finished she thanked him with murderous sweetness for explaining things, because, as a Duquesne, she had never been instructed in tacky tactics. And so that he might understand the code of her world, she said, she wanted him to know that her word had meaning. His refusal to respect her word, after she had told him she wouldn't consider such offers, was offensive. Or would have been, except she knew it was unintentional. Unintentional because, she didn't need to say, he didn't know any better.

The haughty ease with which she put him down had a style the bystanders appreciated. They grinned, some laughed aloud. Penstone's long, but oddly fat-cheeked face, which looked like a huge sly fox with mumps, flushed.

He'd come off a scrubby hill farm and married a widow with good land to get his start and the challenge to his gentlemanly pretensions rankled. A gentleman to the manner born, Nikki thought wryly, might have knocked her teeth out, but George stood there with egg on his face and offered an apology.

Then, with a veiled threat, he reminded her that the landed gentry's day was gone. Only the tough new breed survived. Without such a man's hand her property could not be run profitably. With her permission he'd make one last bid—his top price. She'd told him to go ahead. He'd offered a single dollar more.

Imagining he'd turned the tables and made a fool of her, he laughed, expecting the others to join him. But his sound was grating, his look bullying. It reminded them that Penstone had beaten his two divorced wives, abused other women and was a "back-door husband" to other men's wives. Besides, he was known to have cheated honest men in business deals and he used his money, power and position as a director of the local bank ruthlessly. Fearing him, a few grinned with him, but most of them sided with Nikki. Even those who had long resented her overprivileged background, big land holdings and high-toned ways were on the alert for things to like about a girl who looked like Nikki.

Putting on her shower cap that morning, she accidentally discovered the perfect answer to any future offers by Penstone. Standing with velvet hips tilted to one side, her narrow, tapering upper body to the other, her arms were raised to her head and bent at elbows and wrists. Her deftly moving feminine hands and fingers formed a rapid series of curves as she stuffed her hair into the flowered plastic cap. Her face was turned to one shoulder, and at the same time that she touched one ear with her thumb she glimpsed her naked back in a full-length mirror.

In the future, she thought smolderingly, she'd give Penstone an efficient, wordless reply by thumbing her ear. The gesture would tell him she wasn't listening and also convey another, delicately bitchy, meaning. Nikki shifted her weight quickly from one leg to the other so that her bottom wagged impudently. Then she went in the shower.

Both had frequent business throughout the area and soon, in the normal course of things, their paths would cross again. Penstone, a slugging, stomping brawler till fairly recently, was no man to avoid a possible clash, Nikki was sure. But three times in two weeks when they found themselves approaching each other, he veered off hastily.

To have the bully on the run amused her, but it puzzled her that she could have got under his thick skin so easily. True, she'd humiliated him, but she hadn't dreamed it would unsettle him to such a degree. And it couldn't have, she thought with a slight chill, except that she had touched something much deeper.

She had a brief, dark insight into his whole life. He'd been born into a ragged, shoeless brood existing in a one-room shack on soil too poor to feed them. The struggle for survival at that level, where bare necessities were a luxury, was relentless and grim. Inhabitants of such a world had neither the means nor leisure to cultivate nice manners, nor any desire to please the comfortable world that despised them for their unfortunate lot and called them white trash.

Considering the odds against them it was no wonder so many lost hope, becoming shiftless and drunken, or roused to assert dignity through violent fights, or tried to smash their way out of an intolerable life by crime. Their tomorrows promised little or nothing; they seized what pleasures they could. Their primitive sexual morality was stripped of the romantic frills indulged in by the hateful outside world and defied that world's laws against incest.

Nikki could understand George Penstone abstractly as a symbol of man fighting off oppression to make something of himself. But she saw the flesh-and-blood Penstone coldly as her enemy. That's how he saw her, as a natural enemy, a symbol of everything that had ever oppressed him. Whether or not it was personal, he hated what she represented. And he was out to cause her all the trouble he could and destroy her if possible.

The next time they met he didn't veer off. From his smirk it was obvious he had something up his sleeve. He slowed and spoke her name, expecting her to stop for whatever he had to say. Her plan to thumb her ear was silly, beneath her dignity. Furthermore, she realized, to goad him any more might be dangerous. The next instant Nikki glanced at him and touched her thumb to her ear. She walked on past without a pause, her manner airily unconcerned. But her heartbeat quickened. She wasn't sure he understood.

When she did it next day, there wasn't the slightest doubt that he read her loud and clear. The frozen stare he gave her made the skin on the back of her neck crawl. It was an effort to keep from looking back.

Their next encounter was at the courthouse in the county seat. Penstone was standing just inside an office doorway scowling at some item in a thick real estate title abstract. She came along the basement hall, casual in sweater, blue jeans and mocs, her hair in a swinging ponytail.

Hearing the light feminine rhythm of her step, his down-slanting gaze slid off the edge of the document to her legs. For moments his gaze clung voluptuously to the upper flare of her thighs and lower slope of her belly, then jumped to her breasts. Unmistakably her body excited him; his bulging cheeks rose in a high grin. Finally he looked at her face. He saw whose body he'd been enjoying. His confusion was laughable.

Nikki couldn't resist pausing and murmuring, "Character always trips 'em up when they forget a girl's got a head."

She laughed softly and walked on. Glancing across her shoulder on entering the assessor's office, she saw he was out in the hall, glaring after her.

Nikki left the assessor's office an hour later. Penstone, looking grumpy and sweaty in gray seersucker and yellow straw hat, was up in the foyer near the lunch stand. The moment he saw her he came to the mouth of the hall, swaggering like a rustic Caesar and puffing a cigar. He took a feet-apart stance, half-blocking the passage. Words were choking him and he couldn't wait for her to reach him.

"Let *me* tell *you* a thing or two, Missy . . ." He began.

"Permission granted."

"There you go again, talkin' to me like I'm some no-account!" he exploded. He clamped the cigar in his teeth, glowering. When he was back in control, he thumped his chest and said hoarsely, "I got the *biggest* land holdings of anybody in this county, including you."

She nodded, standing relaxed although she was alert.

"There ain't no smart answer to *that*, huh?" He made a coughing sound of humorless laughter.

"You told me thing one. Let's have thing two."

"Yeah. To me a female's a female, none of 'em special. I get any I want. Don't get no high-nose notion I want *you*. Next . . . who're *you* to talk about anybody's character trippin' them up? I'll tell you whose'll trip who up. Yours, Missy! A flittin' around female like you won't last it out when she finds out runnin' a big farm ain't all fun. You can't never make a paying proposition out of it with your highfalutin ways."

"Penstone," she said tiredly, "I won't do business with you and I want nothing to do with you personally and

I'm not interested in your character or your judgment of mine. So—"

"You still think you can dismiss me like a stable hand!" He said angrily. "Well, you listen good. I'm a director at the bank and we look at character when we consider loans. You can't put your daddy's and great-great-granddaddy's character on the line—just *yours*. And you've lived like a rich, spoiled brat. You got no history whatever of being responsible and settled down or knowing how to handle that money you inherited. You never proved you're big enough to take hold of anything serious and hang on. Oh, you got serious intentions *now*—for a while—but they don't amount to nothing better than female emotions. It's where you was born and reared, so you *wish* it was as good as you think it is!"

She laughed drily. "I could almost admire your ambition to have the *best* instead of merely the *biggest* land holdings in the county. It shows you have at least *some* instinct for quality. Not much. For example, your cigars are rolled from your own tobacco crops," she said, wrinkling her nose and fanning smoke away from her face.

"What's wrong with this cigar? What the hell does a woman know about tobacco—or anything else?"

"About tobacco, this woman knows that when she gets her first crop of burley to the auction sheds it'll outgrade and outdollar yours. Matter of fact, Penstone, acre for acre I'll get a higher yield than you will on any crop or crops you want to name. And I'll bet on it, anywhere from a thousand to a hundred thousand dollars. We'll put the conditions of the bets in writing and put our money in escrow, and winner take all. How about that, Mr. Penstone? Or are you all bluster and bluff?" she challenged, quivering with anger.

He just glared for a moment, then blurted: "You think I'd lock up any money when I could have it working for me? Shows *your* business judgment."

"I'll take your personal note."

"I'm too smart to take yours!"

"What you're too smart for is to make a bet you know you'd lose," she said coldly. "But not smart enough to understand that the offer you made on my place shows your poor judgment of property values. Your top buying price is only half what I'm going to *borrow* on it. So it would be useless for me to try negotiating a loan at a bank you speak for."

He blinked and said hastily, "Now, wait a minute." He shook his head and chuckled. "Oh, you're a high-tempered little thing. You sure can put me on good. Why, now, Miss Duquesne, a smart, college-educated girl like you, that's been around all over the world and held her own, knows good and well how folks in these parts do business. Fussin' and fightin' goes right along with dickerin' and dealin'. Leastways it does among the menfolks. I got no social touch to deal with the ladies in a business way. I admit it." He laughed at himself, falling into the role of an humble, good-natured simpleton. "I guess I'm just a dirt farmer at heart, used to horse-tradin'. Naturally, my private horse trades got nothin' whatever to do with bank business."

"Then you'll have no trouble explaining to your fellow directors why I took my business to Richmond."

She stepped around him and sailed across the foyer and out of the courthouse. Penstone hustled along beside her across the square and to her car, talking jovially all the way. He reinterpreted everything he'd said, laughed at his own "poor boy" manners, flattered her lavishly. She said nothing till she was in her car. Then she looked out at him standing there with his "friendly" grin turned on full cheek and said disgustedly, "Come off of it. You've got no more use for me than I have for you."

His fraudulent grin changed into a leer. His gaze moved over her breasts and down to the crotch of her snug jeans and back up again with slow, bold contempt.

"I'd have *some* use for you," he said nastily.

"I have a use for you, too," she flared. "It keeps me on my toes and it's good for me to have an enemy to trounce. In *that* role you serve me well. But I couldn't use you sexually. I'm very particular. Don't bother to apply again."

"I'm man enough to satisfy the best woman that ever lived. But it'll be a cold day in hell before I give you a break. You're my enemy, too, and before it's over I'll run you out of these parts."

She laughed scornfully, and switched on the engine.

"I'm woman enough to change you from a hater to a would-be lover with his tongue hanging out if I choose," she said. She started the car rolling. "Which I don't. Get out of the way."

Ever since then he'd tried repeatedly to put her down, and ended up pinning his own shoulders. He felt threatened by the possibility of her success. He was agitated by the sight and sound of her tractors and field equipment, of cattle trucks and Kentucky horse vans rolling to her barns, of work progressing smoothly.

Nikki was involved in her own affairs, not with him, so for the most part he carried on their fights all by himself. Her own will to win was strong, his was compulsive and blind, driving him to make a fool of himself.

He went around laughing and jeering at her and proclaiming himself champion. She wouldn't have stopped him if she could because she picked up succulent tidbits of gossip. Such as the time somebody offered him elaborate sympathy over the way he was being riled up and bothered half out of his mind by a mere slip of a girl. It was inhuman the way she didn't care one bit about what she was doing to him—in fact, hardly bothered to notice him. And, Penstone's "sympathizer" gigged him, just like a woman, she took unfair advantage of having better land to start with, and instead of having pity and not trying to shame his place, she just went heartlessly ahead and built her farm up better and better.

His worst mistake was to make loud jokes about her soil study. She detested picture postcard farms with slicked-up, white-fenced fronts and sick backfields. So, having the brains and honesty to know what she didn't know and admit it, Nikki engaged a professor of agronomy and two graduate students to make a month-long comprehensive soil analysis.

Her team of specialists, working with her general foreman, lab men at the experimental station and the county agent, had diagnosed each field individually. They prescribed tons of chemicals and developed long-range crop programs. The soundness of the modern, scientific approach was obvious, but Penstone guffawed about her extravagance and silly female notions that she could "plow with books."

During their stay the men ate and slept in her large house. Penstone passed leering remarks about manless females needing schoolboys and professors to service them.

That one outraged her. She told herself to stay aloof, deny him that satisfaction of knowing he could disturb her. She was above him; she would *not* be dragged down. She began to congratulate herself on her maturity and self-control. But her stomach rebelled. One evening her pleasure in a luscious steak turned to pain. With angry insight she knew that if she kept trying to tame herself and got any more "adult" about this thing she'd end up on an infant's diet, sick with ulcer. The world was divided, she reminded herself, between those who got ulcers and those who caused them.

Next day she nailed him publicly and gave him a taste of the real Nikki in a tongue-lashing so thorough and swift that he couldn't get a word in. She finished him off and stomped away, quivering with excitement.

Soon enough the thriving condition of her crops showed up Penstone, and his land, too. He began to find excuses to drop over. She didn't invite him in the house but he often caught her around a barn or paddock or on a field road and she let him stay because she knew how intensely the fine look of her land aggravated him, and therefore how much he must want her sexually to put up with it.

Every chance he got he pawed her figure with his eyes and contrived with no success at all to "accidentally" get his hands on her. He hated to be caught sneaking looks and she delighted in letting her attention seem to wander and then turn sharply, catching him.

"I used to say," she'd told him once, "that 'Where Nikki is, things happen.' And they do. That's why, these days, since I've come on the scene, everybody around here is keeping an eye on me. The big things are happening on *this* farm, things that everyone can learn from and profit by. By keeping an eye on me," she said casually, then abruptly changed tone. "*I don't mean the crude way you're staring at my skirt!*"

He coughed and admitted grudgingly, "Yeah, I was lookin'. Only you don't know the reason."

"I know the reason. You know the reason. Be man enough to admit it."

"There you go! Well, then, I won't tell you, and what'll happen will happen." He turned and went to his car with an air of injury. "I won't never be back."

But he phoned that evening.

"Miss Duquesne, I thought it over. And despite our personal feelings toward each other, I've got a responsibility. So, to prevent a terrible thing happening I'll tell you what I said I wouldn't."

"All right."

"You see I ain't all bad."

"Nobody is."

"I'm sure glad to hear you say that. And it don't surprise me. A college-educated, quality girl that knows the world has tolerance like that. Not like the ignorant, envious, narrow-minded, closed-in kind of little people around here. What they hate about you and me is we made something of ourselves and they can't stand nothing that's superior to 'em. That's how come they spread stories to cause trouble between you and me. You heard of 'divide and conquer.'"

"I'm hearing it right now—you trying to divide me from people who're friendly to me and not to you. Now, what was it you felt obliged to tell me about, to prevent some terrible thing happening?"

"It's the kind of delicate matter that can't be said over the phone. I'll come on over. Be there in five minutes."

"If you want to call on me in the evening, you'll have to come right out with it and ask for a date."

There was a long pause. Finally he said harshly, "All right! I'll give it to you hard and straight. You got some mean roughnecks among your field hands. The type that don't give a damn about *nothing* if they get steamed up enough. But you keep goin' around 'em, all perfumed up and lookin' silky and actin' gay like a party. You flaunt what you got around. You go driving alone down them back roads of yours out of sight or yellin' distance of help, and they watch you close! You're askin' for it! That plain enough for you?"

"It's plain enough what you're up to. You tried—and don't deny it!—to raid my work crews and couldn't hire them away from me. Now you want to scare me into firing good men." She said it defiantly, but her glance flicked uncertainly toward the massive, yet always unlocked, front door.

"You call it raid. I call it business to be on the lookout for good workers wherever I can get them."

"You have to be on the lookout, the turnover you have. People don't quit *me* all the time," she jeered. She began to pace nervously. She was aware of her aloneness in this big house except for her maid and the cook-housekeeper. She drew a deep, steadying breath. "What did you want with any of my people if they're so terrible?"

"Women!" he nearly exploded. "I never yet seen one that didn't throw out what brains she's got and think with her feelin's in a bad situation."

"What?" She blinked and stopped pacing. What he said was uncomfortably close to the truth. The unsettling thing was to know that this detestable lout was capable of a perception like that.

"You heard me. You won't listen on account of you don't like me or what I got to say. It ain't *nice* what I got to say. It don't make you feel good. So you won't have nothin' to do with it. You always got a smart comeback to keep yourself from hearing what you don't want to. I never said these roughnecks wasn't good *workers*," he snorted. "Sure they are. And I don't have to worry about them like if I was a pretty girl. You think, oh, how they love and respect the nice purty boss lady who don't *never* chew 'em out. She leaves the mean men bosses do all that dirty work for her and goes flaunting what she's got around."

"I do not flaunt. Or tease. Or titillate," she cried out, her voice thin.

"Anyway, there ain't a doubt that you're a constant temptation to 'em."

"I suppose not," she said, uneasily. She was aware of her heart beating rapidly. "I'll concede that you've made some sound general observations."

"You're conceding something for a change?"

"Yes. It's surprising, but on some things you and I think alike. I detest the phony people who won't face reality and try to abolish or deny any truth that's unpleasant. Especially truths about themselves. If I was falling into being that kind of person without realizing it and you've pointed it out—well, I may owe you a thanks."

"You big enough to pay it?" he chuckled.

She stood clenching her teeth and scowling.

"No matter how right some of what you say is," she said finally, "maybe you're bluffing. Trying to bully me till I *will* feel instead of think. Feel scared and act hysterical, and upset the smooth way things are going!"

"So you're not going to do nothing about it?"

"I'll decide."

"Maybe it's a laugh, me thinking you'd be scared," he said insinuatingly. "Knowing their type, I figured you set 'em wild imaginin' that lily-white body naked. I knew they were takin' you to bed regular, but so far just in their minds. I thought, bein' low-lifes that couldn't come courtin' quality like you, that the only way they could get it was rape. Guess I figured wrong."

She began to laugh. "Penstone, for a while back there you had me confused. I was afraid there was a part of you I'd have to respect. You don't know what a relief it is to hear the real, unmistakable you. Now the relationship between me and the men I hire must remain secret. But one thing can be made clear. Rape is the only way *you* could get me. The taking of my lily-white body to bed regularly will have to continue just in your mind."

"Not *my* mind."

"You've got a bad case—can't stay away, can't admit why you hang around. If you admitted, you'd have to *beg* for what you want, and still not get it. You can't begin to imagine how really desirable my body is. Once there was an all-American football player, a mass of muscle who could have picked you up by the scruff of the neck. He couldn't stay away. He put whipped cream all over my body and licked it off with his tongue. And judging by the fervor of current suitors of mine in New York and Paris, the allure of my flesh is—"

Abruptly he hung up the phone. Nikki smiled tightly.

The time came when the affairs of the farm were so well organized that her presence wasn't necessary and Nikki felt free to launch out. Her trips to New York, with an occasional jaunt to Paris, became more frequent. She set up an apartment in New York and spent half her time there, in the company of lively companions, many of them from the theater.

Penstone was as upset about her absences as a jealous, suspicious husband. He couldn't wait to come over and fish around about what she might have been up to. He was sure she had a man—or men—in her life and she certainly didn't deny it. One would have thought she had betrayed him and the whole community. He boasted more and more openly about his sexual prowess and swaggered around showing off, as if expecting her to fall into a sudden swoon and plead with him to make love to her.

Finally, he headed her off by a paddock fence. He glanced over his shoulder to be sure there were no eavesdroppers. His fat cheeks sagged, and there was a kind of sick fever in his eyes and when, with a final bravado, he lit a big cigar his thick hands shook.

When he spoke, he tried to get some aggression in his voice, to convince her *he* had the upper hand and was no supplicant for anybody's favor. The sound had a wounded-animal-bellow quality about it which might have touched her sympathies. But the words were arrogant.

"I want you to go to bed with me."

She rammed her fists on her hips and thrust her face at him.

"I'm not going to take a crude pitch like that. *What did you say?*" she demanded.

"I said I'm crazy about you. I'd like to . . . like to . . . love you. I mean there's no use to kid each other. We're grown up. You're one helluva woman and I want you."

"That's better," she said. "But I don't want you."

"I admit I been wrong in a lot of things. But I want to make it up."

"Drop the subject."

He kept at it, though. Every time he came around he propositioned her bluntly. She didn't mind the straight approach, but she loathed him, and kept chasing him off. He'd got the right idea that she wasn't merely playing hard to get and he didn't like it a damned bit.

Actually, of the hundred-odd guests in her orchard that spring morning he alone was unwelcome. But he'd pushed himself to the forefront. As Nikki mounted a crate in front of the bee truck, his gaze was crudely fixed on her bare legs. She delicately placed the toe of her sandal on the thick black shadow of his head there on the crate and bore down, turning her pretty, high-arched foot as though mashing out a cigarette. Penstone got the message. He glanced up, frowned and shifted his position. Nikki gave him a brief, haughty look, then smiled radiantly at the crowd.

Chapter Two

"Good morning, everybody. This is such a good turnout it's a shame I'm not running for office," Nikki said buoyantly. She paused to enjoy their good-natured laughter, then continued in a rush of words, her high, clear feminine voice warm with enthusiasm. "I'm *very* happy to see all of you—pardon, I mean 'you all'—including my favorite uncles and aunts and cousins, kissin' and otherwise, and old acquaintances, neighbors and friends of mine and of my dad's and mother's."

Unexpectedly she touched an emotionally tender area in herself and faltered. She rallied at once.

"First, for the benefit of the few of you I missed at the main gate, let me repeat: When this demonstration is over, we're having a big buffet breakfast up at the house. Whether you eat it or drink it, there'll be something to suit your taste. And plenty of it, because Nikki's her father's daughter and she's not about to break that tradition of his. You come now, because you'll enjoy it and I'll be proud to have you. So don't you go 'way. Hear?"

She deliberately lapsed into a Southern idiom and rhythm, her words slowing to a lazy-sweet drawl that was both mocking and affectionate. She felt a fullness and richness in her breast, a surging of good will. She wanted it to reach out and touch and bind them all. Her gaze roamed over the crowd, her pleasure in them clear, as was their responsive pleasure in her. It was an exalted moment, inexpressibly beautiful, as if all that was good and fine within her and them had fused together with the total atmosphere of this spring morning, so clean and bright and fragrant with apple blossoms.

Nikki was quick with life and excited by the meaning of the occasion. This new pollination method blended ancient folk knowledge of bee culture with pure research and modern technology to produce a sort of miracle. Her enthusiasm for the advanced technique had infected the proprietor of the local professional bee service and now she was going to be the first to introduce it in this area.

It thrilled her because the technique in itself was great, and because it was happening where it should, on Duquesne land, and because she was Nikki and loved to be out there in front tasting victory while her enemy was swallowing one more bitter dose.

"Now to business." She half-turned, raising her bare arm in a flowing gesture that included the bee truck behind her and its unsmiling, leathery-faced proprietor standing by one fender. "We all know Mr. Lauder. We've been contracting for the services of his Tri-County Commercial Bee Company to pollinate our apple and peach orchards for as long as I can remember. He's an expert on bees. And such a hard-headed businessman that it would be as impossible to get him carried away by newfangled ideas as it is to make him smile."

A burst of laughter from the crowd made Nikki turn to see the sober Mr. Lauder grinning.

"What am I going to do with you? I thought you'd be on your best behavior," she scolded, tongue in cheek, and looked at him sadly. He grinned wider. Suddenly he chuckled aloud and announced:

"She tickles me! She gets as worked up about things as a little kid. It gives you a lift." He shook his head, then began to frown. "Don't let me give the wrong idea about her. There's a gent around here," he said drily, giving Penstone an unfriendly glance, "who has remarked about this modern pollination technique that it was a sort of toy likely to fascinate a wild-headed girl. The application of electronics to known procedures doesn't amount to a toy. Miss Duquesne wouldn't fool with it if it did, because she's smart as a whip. And she's not standing up there doing the talking just to let you see how pretty she is but because she can explain it better than I can."

She smiled at him, feeling genuinely touched.

"You're really nice, Mr. Lauder."

"I like you," he said simply. "Go on."

She briefly summarized what had been known about honeybees till 1947.

". . . Then von Frisch's experiments in Munich solved the mystery of how a bee bringing sugar back to the hive tells other bees exactly where the source is. Von Frisch set out sugar water in various locations ranging from ten yards to two miles from the hive. He marked certain bees specifically so that he knew where each was getting its sugar. He inserted a pane of red glass into the hive and observed the interior.

"He saw that the returning worker bee performed dances on the wall of the comb while the other bees crowded around. These dances were not haphazard. There were circlings in one direction or another a certain number of times; or figure eights; or straight-line movements up, down, across or at a particular angle diagonally; and reverse movements, repetitions, tail waggings, variations of tempo from fast to slow.

"Every element had its precise meaning and conveyed some bit of accurate information. Bees that hadn't known of the sugar source were able to fly in the proper direction for the correct distance and find it easily.

"Imagine! It was true that bees had a language. Isn't that, and the fact that a man learned to understand it, marvelous?" Nikki asked rhetorically, then directly. "It really is marvelous, isn't it?"

She nodded her head, prompting the crowd who were listening with serious interest. Some nodded with her, others smiled, sharing her appreciation. Penstone was sucking his cheeks in to keep from laughing, she noted with a flicking glance before continuing.

"The dance message differed according to the time of day, even though there was no change in the location of the sugar source. This showed that the instructions about direction of sugar source depended on more than its relationship to the hive. The other factor was the position of the sun in the sky. The bees set their compasses to the sun."

"How come, then," Penstone broke in, "that they know where to go when there's so much clouds they couldn't see through 'em?"

"Well, Mr. Penstone," she said flippantly, "as the carnival spieler said when his stooge called out a question, 'I'm mighty glad you asked that, sir.' The answer is in the structure of the bee's eye, each of which has four thousand lenses—and no, sir, I did not personally count 'em. The complex eye structure effects a polarization of the light. As long as there's *some* clearing somewhere in the sky the bee can locate the sun. An explanation of the polarization of light is not a part of my present lecture, sir."

She laughed, than frowned. "Sorry. I don't mean to be patronizing. I realize many of you know all about what I've already said and am going to say. But others don't, and I want to make the picture clear for everybody.

"Let's move on a dozen years to 1959 and Dr. Wolfgang Steche, also of Munich. He made a toy. An artificial bee. He affixed it to the comb wall inside a hive. By electronic controls he manipulated this bee so that it performed a meaningful dance. The real bees clustered around and received instructions, sensing the motions, picking up the delicate vibrations through their feet. Within minutes the real bees were mobilized. They flew to the source of sugar, which they had never seen before.

"When you think about it, it seems fantastic. But true. It happened. Subsequently there was much experimentation, observation and study. Inevitably, the technologists got to work, automation techniques of programming were applied. Coded tapes were made, which would activate the artificial bee in any dance pattern required. Mr. Lauder has this modern equipment and a selection of tapes and has only to choose the appropriate one, switch his switches and send a whole hive wherever he wants it to go.

"In the natural course of affairs the scouts would have to fly out to investigate possible sources of nectar, and fly back and report. Time is wasted. Weather's often a problem. Whole blocks of trees can be missed. The advantages of this system are obvious. Now, except for the control mechanism there in the cab of the truck, everything that goes on is out of sight.

"On the surface the procedure will look familiar. The troughs at the entrances of the hives are filled with pollen. When the doorways are opened, the bees will have to walk through the pollen before they can take flight. Each will, of course light on a tree's flower and get the nectar it needs and in the process the flower gets what it needs, the pollen from the bee's legs. Not a passionate mating, but an entirely proper beginning for such a wholesome fruit as an apple, I'm sure," she said, grinning.

"Mr. Lauder is about ready, I think. He will demonstrate with Hive No. 1. The tape he uses will electronically activate the artificial bee on the wall inside that hive. The code on the tape will tell the live bees to fly south and west for 350 yards to a certain tree. The trunk of that tree has been marked for us and presently we'll go to it. The bees will go there and pollinate that tree and their overflow will light in adjacent trees. They will fly past many other flowering trees more convenient to the hive and equal or superior as sources of nectar."

She glanced around, looked questioningly at Mr. Lauder sitting in the truck cab at the control mechanism box. He nodded.

"All right," Nikki called. "Hive No. 1 is in the bottom row of hives at the front of the truck bed there on the right side. Let's move around to that side and spread out in a semicircle, not too close in. I think we can all see well enough."

The crowd shifted and took positions to watch the hive entrance. Almost at once the first bee appeared, waded through the trough full of fine pollen and took off. It was followed immediately by another and another in an unbroken stream of dozens, and eventually hundreds, of bees. They flew up in an ascending spiral, their bodies a line of diminishing dots vanishing far above the trees in a southwesterly direction.

One after another of the men set off in the same direction, squinting regularly at the sky spaces between trees. Soon, most of the crowd was on the move. Nikki began to go with them, her pace erratic, slowing to walk and talk with someone for a few paces, then spurting ahead to join another. By the time she reached the marked tree a double rank of men surrounded its perimeter, staring up or exchanging quiet remarks. Nearly every one of them turned to her with big smiles.

From the tree's crest of white blossoms came the great, droning hum of the bees. She felt runs of quick little thrills over the warm sensitive skin of her whole body and her breasts tingled. She drew a deep breath, blinking back tears of joy, and her face sparkled with loveliness. *Honey thunder,* she thought, a beautiful sound!

Mr. Lauder endured a plague of questions, then became deaf and dumb. He consulted a tree map and got on with the job of pollinating the whole orchard. Clearly the show was over.

Nikki led the way to the main house. She detoured slightly to pass the line of workers' houses, greenhouses, a field of young, lettuce-green tobacco, patches of it covered with "tobacco canvases," strips of heavy white muslin. The barns were open and most of the thoroughbred mares and foals were outside in the paddocks or larger pasture. The sight of them grazing or walking or running at an easy lope for the sheer pleasure of it never failed to delight her and she slowed a little, watching. There were chocolate bays and near-black browns and reddish chestnuts with silver manes and their coats gleamed in the sunlight and rippled with the underlying play of finely coordinated muscle.

The gawky, leggy, knobby-kneed young colts and fillies rarely got far from their mothers. They were capable of solemn conduct but subject to fits of exuberance. For no apparent reason they might hop straight up in the air and whirl around or plunge away, flinging their heads from side to side, or caper and prance and kick up their heels, often ending in a comical sprawl.

The mares lifted their heads, ears pricking, and sighted the motorcade and came running to the fence, their foals laboring mightily and uselessly to keep pace. They reached the fence and ran away or raced along beside the cars or just stood, curious but wary. The foals, their coats still fuzzy, pressed as close to the mama as possible. One huge-eyed little bay with a white blaze on his forehead insisted, despite his mother's annoyed efforts to shake him by moving repeatedly, on stationing himself between her forelegs.

Brood mares, with their seasons at the race tracks behind them, automatically stood to a stallion as soon as they came to heat after foaling, and these had been pregnant when Nikki bought them. Some had already been covered again, this time by one of her own two stallions. Only one of the mares had aborted; the foal crop was a good one, she was sure. Or as sure as anyone could be. She hadn't bought blind, but studied their bloodlines, top line and mare line, too.

Still, the proof of a race horse was on the track. These foals couldn't start to race for two years, even assuming they showed, in training, that they could run. And by their very nature, these lovely creatures, with strength and hardiness bred out of them for the sake of speed, were unusually nervous and vulnerable to all sorts of injuries and sicknesses.

Food and shelter and vet services aside, there was the expense of a good horse barn foreman, trustworthy grooms and, later, training jockeys and a trainer. Added to the whopping initial price, this crop of appealing horseflesh would be her biggest single investment. And she knew it was a long-shot gamble at best.

Well, she'd done it. She couldn't undo it, at this stage, without a big loss. Still, it should have taught her to go easy. It was true, as even her lawyer, and best friend, warned, that her money was not limitless.

Nonetheless, only two months ago she'd let herself get enthused about something she couldn't even claim to know anything about. And she had put a *fortune* into the riskiest venture known to mankind—backing a Broadway play. What on earth had she been thinking about to gamble that kind of money and jeopardize this whole property and her very home? Well, there was a time to worry, and the time wasn't now. She had hungry, thirsty guests. She parked and walked up to the main house.

The three-story forty-room Georgian-style mansion with a total of sixteen fluted white columns along its broad front and two side verandas sat on a knoll which was the highest point of land for miles. Built in 1893, it featured a ballroom, banquet room, large parlors with ornate cabinetwork, a huge kitchen. It had been a fine example of conspicuous display by her great-grandfather, a scoundrel who had spent his life in conspicuous acquisition of mills, mines, timberland, rail and shipping lines—and "fancy women," according to his *un*authorized biography.

He had a fifty-year-old son (Nikki's grandfather) a scrupulous man who lost half the family holdings when he built the house as a wedding gift for a twenty-year-old bride! The moralists hopefully predicted sudden death for him. And a year later they were proven right in the wrong way. It wasn't sexual overexertion but sexual deprivation and temper that felled him. She began giving her favors to younger men and withholding them from him and he got into such jealous rages he had a fatal stroke.

In her sober moments Nikki was ashamed of him. He'd been ruthless, underhanded and dishonest in his business dealings, using graft and bribery, corrupting officials and legislators. In league with other financiers, he'd brought ruinous economic pressures to bear on competitors. In short, he was a crook, big and shifty enough to stay out of prison and get rich, rich enough to give his son and his son's son and Nikki herself a life of luxury. He'd given her financial security, relieved her of all need to claw and scramble and made possible her fine education. She became so enlightened that she could despise him morally. What an irony! that everything she was privileged to be resulted from the villainy that she condemned.

Sometimes she had to laugh sourly at her own pretensions. She owed him *some* feeling of loyalty or gratitude, but she refused it. She tried to deny all feeling of kinship, and couldn't. There were times, such as now, going with her guests to eat and drink in his house, when she couldn't help a perverse sort of pride about one thing at least. The way he had died. The old devil hadn't gone out with a whimper, but fighting mad.

The house came alive in the next hour. The talk and laughter and good eating had a party spirit that absorbed her and she enjoyed the hostess role. More had come than she expected; tables in the banquet-hall, dining room, sun room and kitchen seated only sixty. She had to get some of the others set on benches, sofas, chairs, even stair steps. Fortunately, quite a few preferred to eat on the move anyhow. Carts and warmers and trestleboard tables around three walls of the banquet hall displayed the food mouth-wateringly and in abundance that was a pleasure in itself.

There were platters of eggs, fried and scrambled, grilled beefsteaks, ham steaks, sausage, bacon, liver, hot biscuits and gravy, toast, muffins, mounds of butter, jams, jellies, juices, hot cereals, fried mush, hotcakes, syrups, two deep crocks heaped with strawberries, half-gallon pitchers of pure cream, and for the pie-for-breakfast faction she'd provided four different varieties. Three farm girls and a maid were helping the cook and they constantly replenished serving dishes and bowls, milk pitchers and coffeepots.

Nikki ate in snatches, moving in and out of all the rooms, attaching herself to one and another group, for a few personal words and to make sure they were taken care of. Decanters of liquor, mixers, ice and glasses had been set out on a sideboard and a good proportion of the men had drinks. Among the straight whisky drinkers was Penstone. In her house he was a guest like any other, so she was pleasant.

But before long she noticed he was drinking too much and his attention to her was becoming too fixed. Whenever she crossed the room his eye never left her and he missed nothing, from her red-lacquered toenails and bare legs to the bright gloss of her hair.

The occasion had overstimulated her and she was already feeling that pleasant tingle of sensuality which was on the very edge of hot sexual cravings. She didn't want to be made any more intimately conscious of herself. She gave him a fretful look of displeasure. Next time she passed by he pawed her with his eyes again. She gave him a sharper glance. He just grinned slackly, took a big breath and turned to get another drink.

He was burning for her. She knew it. She felt the powerful male force of it. For an instant she was aware of his mass and thrust. The thought flashed in her mind that he was all man. She flushed.

It disturbed her badly to think that he could rouse desire in her. A little frightened, Nikki assured herself that *she* could not have responded to *him*. It had only been a case of an instinctive femaleness responding to impersonal virile male force, she thought indignantly.

She frowned. Righteous indignation aside, she scoffed at herself, she *had* responded. So face it.

She was scarcely aware that Penstone had followed her. He cornered her and said, "I'd give twenty of my best acres to bed a wild mare like you!"

"Which twenty?" she asked tartly and at the same time she slapped his face hard and loud.

He blinked. He gaped. Dumb astonishment, then flashing rage, then a huge grin touched his face. Nikki's palm print began to show like a brand. With a lazy sway Nikki shifted her balance and stood with feet apart, fists resting on her hips. Then she just stared at him. So did thirty other people.

Penstone's face became redder by the moment. Grinning, he looked to the right, to the left. He looked back at her and chuckled. Nikki simply continued to stare.

"You got a wallop!"

He laughed loudly. Nikki maintained a regal "We are not amused" expression. His false heartiness began to drain away. Obviously he wanted to be elsewhere, anywhere. But he couldn't bring himself to turn tail and run. He stayed, trying to hold onto a remnant of his grin. Someone, then another, laughed.

Penstone squirmed. Nikki enjoyed his discomfort and increased it, drawing a deeper breath than necessary and defining the lovely contours of her high breasts more clearly. With cool amusement she gave the screw another delicate twist. She tapped her foot impatiently and the quick beat and light brush of her knee and thigh inside her skirt agitated the material. In his feverish condition Penstone couldn't be unaware of the teasing motion, nor stare at it directly. While her body lured him her face rejected him disdainfully.

He began to backstep, fumbling out some words about her misunderstanding him, then mentioning an appointment he had. Nikki just watched, silent. Penstone turned around and moved toward the door, balkily at first as if he were being shoved and resisting. Then he practically fled from the house, followed by roaring laughter.

One of the men watching him hurry to his car exclaimed about his speed: ". . . a furlong in ten:three!" This set off volleys of ribald comments about "poor old

George." They joked that Nikki had turned him into a speed horse, saddled him, made him manageable by gelding him, ended his prospects of a career at stud, and even ruined him for service as a "teaser" stallion.

People who had neither heard what she and Penstone said nor seen her slap him relayed exact details of the encounter to others in the next room. A blown-up version got back to her in a few minutes. Her tall, handsome cousin Claude, who had her father's name and much of his looks and charm, weaved through a circle of admirers surrounding her, and said:

"Hi, Cousin Nikki. I hear you're winner and still champ. Slapped him a right and a left, clawed and punched his face, kneed him, spun him around and kicked him all the way to the door, and he's headed for the doc's. Right?" He grinned.

"Wrong. He went to a vet. Seriously, Claude, you know darned well I didn't get rough. I just slapped him. Once. He asked for it."

"He did?" He leered. "That's what I figured."

"I meant the *slapping*'s what he asked for," she cried, and burst out laughing. She pushed him playfully. "Claude, you big old fool. I never should've let a weakheaded boy like you come to the orchard and hear all that racy stuff about the bees and flowers."

"Say, Rex . . . Tom . . . Ed, did you know my purty girl cousin Nikki is going to star in a Broadway play?"

"Say!"

"I'll be there!"

"When, Nikki?"

"Never. Don't pay any attention to Claude. I'm no actress!"

"You're no actress! Oh, boy!"

"I'm not! Outside of some college theatricals and a few weeks at a drama workshop I've had no experience. That column item you saw was just publicity. One of the actresses had walked out. I read her part at a few rehearsals. The producer-director wanted me to take the role. But I'm backing that play and damned if I want any amateurs getting up on that stage and jeopardizing *my* investment. Including me. Besides," she added wryly, "the role was only the second female lead. Not the star part."

"*That* explains it. When's it going to open?"

She rolled her eyes and turned up a palm. "*If* the two stars haven't killed each other or the director, or he hasn't killed them, or if they haven't all joined forces to strangle the playwright, or if *he* hasn't killed *them* all, or himself, *maybe*—unless *I* butcher the lot of them when I go to New York tomorrow night—*possibly* we'll get to Philadelphia for a tryout within a week. *Assuming* we survive that city, then weather a run in New Haven, after which we *might* open in New York in a month."

"Nikki, I hope you've got yourself a big hit, that's what I hope," Claude said, soberly.

"Why, Claude, honey, you say that so sweetly I'm going to give you a kiss for it." She kissed and hugged him quickly.

A bystander declared, "Nikki, every single one of us, beginning with me, hopes you've got yourself a big hit."

"That's so sweet I'm going to give you . . . tickets."

"The only trouble," Claude said, "is that it's been nice having you back home. With a big hit show, even you'll be kept hustling to spend it all. You won't have time for around here."

"Claude! You've got me all wrong," she cried. "It's around here that counts. Not Broadway! You see what I've done for my land. Doesn't it show what it means to me? You can't think I've just been fooling around."

"Not fooling around, Nikki. But you could have done the great job you've done here just because you're a gutty kid and to you a challenge is meat, potatoes and pie. Maybe now that you've licked the biggest problems here, the place won't hold you. Not against a pull like the theater world has."

She shook her head vigorously. "No. This is my world and I love it. It's real. The other's ninety percent fake. It's all dazzle, flash and emptiness." Her eyes shadowed and her voice lowered. "I'm in it like a gambler. And to tell you the truth I'm in too deep."

"With a big Hollywood name like Kris Drake starring in the play, it ought to go strong. Shouldn't it?"

"We hope. We're counting on his big-name pull. How strong it will be, how long his mere glamour will keep audiences coming, who knows? The play's a beauty. But the playwright's unknown. The producer-director hasn't had a solid hit in four-five years, in spite of or because of the fact he's a near-genius. A highly publicized name was needed. And so, Kris Drake," she said unenthusiastically. "In a way it was hedging the bet to use him, instead of a really good, but lesser known, actor. Playing it across the board instead of smacking it all on the nose.

"The role requires a good actor. Essentially Kris Drake is a *personality*. A profile. Pretty boy. A male sex symbol. Kris tries; he *wants* to be an actor. He's never had the chance. Never had his teeth in a demanding role. His confidence is shaky. Twice he's tried to quit. I had a helluva time stopping him. He really takes handling."

"Do you do it like you did to that kid when you were thirteen?" Claude grinned at her slyly.

For an uneasy moment she studied him. She wondered if her personal maid had disobeyed her strict orders never to mention that physical whipping she'd given Kris Drake not two months ago. But she realized Claude was joking.

"Well, hardly," she said, laughing easily.

"Tom," he laughed, "you weren't around here when she was thirteen. You never heard about that whuppin' she gave a boy. He was her age or more, and a full head taller. Nikki had begun to fill out real nice and was in the habit of running around bare-legged in shorts. This kid hanging around the riding stables kept sneaking looks at her, and he teased her that he had a horse could beat her favorite. So, she beat him horse-racin'. Then she hopped him and wrestled him down. Only he enjoyed being put down by a pretty girl like her. That riled her up. Next day, out she marched with her chest bound flat as a boy's and demanded he fight her. He wouldn't fight a girl for real. How'd you get him to, Nikki?"

"A few well-placed insults," she laughed. "He got boiling mad."

Claude went on. "Anyway, the champ here actually whipped him. Put him on his back and sat on him. He couldn't throw her. He yelled and kicked and it didn't do him a bit of good. He got raging and crying, then bawling. Getting beat and sat on by a girl was

33

a disgrace. He begged to get up, but wouldn't admit he was downed. Nikki just made him stay—couple of hours, I think—till he yelled it out loud and clear who was boss. He got up and took out, tail between his legs, like he never wanted to show his face again. Only he did, didn't he?"

She shrugged. "It's embarrassing."

"Listen to her. Embarrassing! Why, she walked around high and proud like she not only owned the land and sky but him, too. She had tamed him and he liked it. He kept coming around to be bossed. He came to the right party. She had him fetch and carry and run errands on the double. And she didn't give him as much as a smile. Even a dog might've got a pat on the head. That poor devil. Nikki, honey, how could you be that mean?"

He and the others laughed with her, but there was a half-serious note in his question.

"If I had it to do today," she said decisively, "I'd be *meaner*. I wouldn't let the worm have the pleasure of being stepped on. Because that's what people like that want; and it's too good for them. I despise anybody who's got no more self-respect than that." She flashed an impish grin. "On the other hand, there are men who've got too damned much ego. Like Penstone. He hates like poison to be put down. So I put him down every chance I get!"

"You be careful of him, though, Nikki. He's a mean son-of-a-bitch. You watch yourself with him. Hear?"

Guests began to leave shortly after ten; by eleven fewer than twenty remained. Among them were men with years of practical experience in land management and animal husbandry problems. Nikki mined them for nuggets of information by encouraging them to indulge in one of their favorite sports: talking. They were glad to give something of value in return for her hospitality and whatever they'd learned in her orchard.

She enjoyed their talk among themselves and to her as much as they enjoyed her genuine interest. Some knew the history of certain fields better than she did and a group of them rode down with her to look them over and offer advice.

A dozen were still there for lunch. Afterward they

all went out to inspect her stock and barns. She urged the interested ones to wander around all they pleased and to count on staying for dinner with her if they could spare the time.

She was reluctant to break away and drive back to the house a little before two o'clock. But she had a special appointment with Vic Hollister, or rather an appointment which was special because it *was* with Vic.

Chapter Three

Vic Hollister was not only her lawyer and friend; he came closer than anyone ever had to Nikki's image of the ideal man. For him she always wanted to look her best. This involved not only a costume flawless for the occasion but time for a refreshing nap. Too often she was late for appointments with him. Today, though, she wasn't due at his office in the county seat till three-thirty, so she had plenty of time.

Yet she entered the house in her habitual rush, aware of needing to slow down, but not slowing. Going to the stairs, she scanned the house appreciatively. Everything had been restored to order, blinds and drapes adjusted to admit a pleasantly hushed light to the fine spacious rooms and broad, curving staircase. Except for distant workaday sounds from the kitchen all was quiet.

She hurried into her third-floor rooms, taking her blouse off. She flung it on a chair, unhooked her bra, glanced at the change of clothes her maid had laid out, removed her Italian sandals in two kick steps and unzipped her skirt while crossing the large, coolly furnished corner bedroom.

In the bathroom she dropped skirt and panties to the floor and went naked on tiptoe to the immense tub, a hollowed-out block of polished gray marble, set on a carpeted platform.

The maid, Mrs. Reed, helped her in, adjusted the head rest, swung the tray of bath things within reach and switched on the ventilator fan. Then, while Nikki reclined idly for two or three minutes, Mrs. Reed stationed herself on a low stool beside a tableful of hairdressing paraphernalia at the head of the tub and waited.

The big, homely personal maid had a passion for all the feminine, pretty things that nature had made her unsuitable for. She adored Nikki's imported intimate undergarments, nightgowns and negligees with their sheerness, froufrou and laces; her hose, shoes, expensive gowns, furs, jewels and tantalizing perfumes. To touch, to launder, to care for her things, to attend the body they ornamented, was a labor of love. While not an outright lesbian, she'd been for years the maid of actresses on the West Coast. It was her joy, almost her mission in life, to submit herself selflessly, not to say worshipfully, to beautiful women.

In the five weeks she had been with Nikki Mrs. Reed had proved she was happy serving her. Mrs. Reed was a gift from Kris Drake. Other lovers might try to express appreciation for sexual favors with jewelry, which was as unacceptable to Nikki as cash. Kris offered a rare sort of gift which he believed would hold an irresistible appeal to her taste for personal power. Through the gift he thought he had outmaneuvered his arch-rival, Anton Bromley, who was directing him in the play and beating his time with Nikki.

In his witless way Kris imagined he was understanding her and cleverly manipulating her. Unfortunately, that was his trouble as an actor—he had little insight. He didn't even guess that Mrs. Reed was his surrogate, that she functioned in the near-slave role he himself craved, just as he'd craved that beating.

He wasn't the man Anton was. And Anton was nothing, really, not compared to Vic Hollister. She sighed.

Nikki lay passive in the warm, delicately perfumed water, listening to the fan's hum. The air flow dispersed the wisps of steam and the water was as clear as a lens, showing her body glowingly white against the dark, intricately patterned marble.

Thinking about Vic, her eyes became dreamily unfocused and her mouth relaxed into a soft pout. She glided one foot back along the floor of the tub a few inches till the rounded point of her knee emerged glossily and began to move her leg languorously from side to side. Her hips rolled slightly with the motion and her lovely conical breasts swayed imperceptibly in the clear, warm water, their pointed colored tips like flower buds.

Slow, invisible currents of water moved over her sensitive bare skin, shaping themselves like lovers' caresses to the exquisite feminine contours of her whole body. Her usually detached awareness of her own beauty and desirability became intense. If only it were all for Vic! She had a sense of inner slackening, of will-less drifting and weakness. She was a woman, Nikki thought in a trance of voluptuousness, with a woman's loving need to serve, to surrender her identity to a man, to a master.

To a master? Nikki raised her eyebrows, lifted her head, hoisted her upper body out of the insidious warm water. She sat slimly erect, her wet, shining breasts thrusting, and thought, *I do the mastering*.

The instant Nikki sat up, Mrs. Reed, knowing her will and obedient to it without command, set to work on her hair. Frowning, Nikki reached for cleansing cream, slapped on gobs of it and spread it over her face and neck. She left the cream on while she attended the rest of her body with lather, brush and wash muff, her face under its slick coating as expressionless, remote and forbidding as a primitive young goddess.

She was imperiously aware of the homely, bony maid working anxiously, maintaining contact with her moving head with remarkable agility and great difficulty. The hands, arms, nerves, mind and whole body of the older, larger woman were forced to adjust to the slightest shift of her own head, she knew with satisfaction.

"You're pulling my hair!" Nikki reprimanded her.

They both knew it was Nikki's fault, but she answered cravenly, "I'm sorry, ma'am!"

"See that it doesn't happen again!"

"Yes, ma'am!"

Nikki removed the cleansing cream. Mrs. Reed finished her hair, an upswept basket weave of crisscrossing strands over the crown of her head finished off by a French twist in back. Nikki stood up and Mrs. Reed rinsed her with the hose and nozzle spray.

Stepping out, Nikki took a towel and began drying

her arms. Mrs. Reed got another towel and went to work on her body, sinking gradually down into a kneeling position, where, finishing, she carefully slipped black satin mules onto her feet.

Nikki stood in the black satin mules looking at her hair-do in the mirror while the maid began to apply spray to set it. The woman glanced at her hoping for a word of approval. Nikki returned the glance indifferently. She lifted her arms, elongating her whole body exquisitely, and Mrs. Reed applied a throat-to-ankle mist of perfume. Then, taking a massive puff, she lightly powdered her whole body, moving in a spiral down and around her while Nikki remained perfectly motionless. Nikki lowered her arms, motioned vaguely and the woman hurried to the little dressing room rack and brought a white, silver-laced negligee as sheer as hosiery.

With the maid following and picking up the clothing she'd strewn across the bedroom, Nikki left the bathroom for her dressing table to make up her face. She looked at it in the mirror directly, then in full and half profile, turning her head slowly to one side and the other. Using a hand mirror, she looked at the sides and back of her hair, precisely but softly coiffed and as vivid as a burst of fire above the smooth white nape of her neck. With narcissistic pleasure she gazed at her face and began to apply cosmetics.

Finishing, she crossed to the chaise and slipped off her satin mules. She settled regally on cushions covered in dark blue velvety fabric, her legs extended, upper body resting against the incline.

Mrs. Reed spread a towel under her lower legs and sat on an ottoman at her feet. From a cart she took lotion and began to stroke it on her feet and ankles and up to her knees. Her touch was easy and soft. She kept her head lowered but now and then she fawningly lifted her eyes to Nikki's. Nikki stared blankly until she dropped her gaze again. The maid uncapped a bottle of polish, applied a careful dot to a chip on one toenail. Then, leaning down, she blew delicately, her lips pursed.

"Are you," Nikki said silkily, "going to kiss it?"

"Would you like that?"

"Only if you'd hate it," she said lazily. "Now get that towel and stuff, including yourself, out of here. I'm going to have a nap."

"Yes, ma'am. What time shall I come back to dress you?"

"I'm dressing myself. I'll let you know when I want you. It'll be hours, maybe not till tomorrow."

Nikki leaned her head back and closed her eyes. She listened until the maid let herself out into the hall and shut the door, then let herself relax totally. She drifted off, setting a mental alarm clock for fifteen—no, twenty minutes. She felt herself dropping peacefully away. She half-roused, hearing a step in the little sitting room connected with this room. Evidently the maid had gone in there from the outer hall for some reason.

Aggravated by the disturbance she promised herself —again!—to fire her the minute they got back to New York. Pay Kris off for what he'd paid her, give her a month's wage and be done with it. She was a corrupting force.

A minute, or maybe two or three later, a whisky scent teased Nikki's nostrils. *Damn it*, she thought, she wouldn't wait to fire her! She drank entirely too often. It was disgusting . . . or pitiful. Maybe the poor creature needed help. But what the devil was she doing here?

Nikki opened her eyes.

There stood George Penstone!

The abrupt sight of him towering over her at the foot of the chaise stopped her breath. She blinked, puzzled for a split second by the position of his hands.

One thumb and forefinger were pincered together.

Holding, she realized with shock, the tab of his zipper! It was still closed.

But Penstone had been preparing to mount her as she slept.

She was in panic. She wanted to leap up and run.

But the instant her body tensed for action, his hands flew out to his sides. His fists clenched.

He crouched and weaved slightly, ready to jump and strike from either side. He was flushed and breathing through his mouth. The vaguely comic fatness of his cheeks was irrelevant to the central foxlike cunning of his face. His eyes were fierce and watchful.

Involuntarily she opened her mouth to scream.

His voice chopped at her: "Shut up!"

There was a spurt to her already quickened heartbeat, a sudden stutter to its rhythm. She closed her mouth, wet her lips. He was deadly. A bludgeoning force, inflamed by whisky and lust and the stings of her many humiliations.

Nikki remained motionless, her senses rawly alert to that brute mass above her. With a flicking glance she noted that in his clenched-fist mood there was a little relaxation of his sexual intensity. His intimidating stare did not waver from her face, and for these few seconds her body didn't exist for him.

While napping she had rolled partially onto her left hip and drawn up that leg. Her negligee had fallen away revealing her satiny inner thigh naked from the bend of her knee to the intimate area of her crotch, and her left breast was totally bare. The transparent white negligee with its open filigrees of silver lace over the sensual flare of her upturned hip was not concealment but added enticement.

His gaze dipped to her body. His hands quickly unclenched and started toward his trousers.

"That will be enough of that!" Nikki said decisively, though her voice was thin and shaky. She covered herself as much as possible and stared at him haughtily. "You're not in the back of a truck or wallowing in a ditch, but in my home!"

"And your home's a palace. A castle. You're the empress," he said bitterly. "Sitting here on her royal couch with a slave at her feet."

'So you were in there hiding and peeping. A drunken Peeping Tom," she said scornfully. "Now, if you've looked your fill, go home and sober up."

"I'm going to have you!"

She looked at his trousers, then curiously at his face. He glanced hastily down at himself, then looked at her suspiciously.

"What are you thinking?" he demanded.

"While you're hating me, you don't want me sexually. Tell me what happens with rapists. Does the love and hate fuse in the sex act? Or is the hate gone once the man has beaten or frightened the girl into submission? It's an act of love, really, isn't it? The violence is in the service of that love. Is that how it is with rape, Penstone?"

"I'm no rapist!" he protested.

"You'll have to be if you're going to have me."

"I don't *want* to hurt you. I don't want this damned fighting between us. I want to love you, damn it. And you keep hitting me every way you can. Fighting me."

"And beating you," she said slashingly. "And driving you out of your mind. Imagine! A grown man, invading my home, my very bedroom, in this way. What's wrong with you?"

"You know!" he said, his face contorted.

"You want me that much? You risk going to jail. You want me that much?" she repeated, peering at him closely.

"I don't give one goddamn about what happens afterward!"

"Penstone," she said shaking her head slowly, "I've got to admit I'm impressed with anybody who can feel that strongly about anything. Anybody who'd risk jail and the position he's built up is crazy, but I can understand, maybe even admire him. However, you can't have me. I don't want you. Far from letting you make love to me, I wouldn't even let you touch me."

He stood frowning at nothing and trembling slightly.

"On the other hand," Nikki said, "I will let you touch me."

His eyes widened. She pointed to the ottoman.

"Sit down."

He nodded and sat and looked at her, waiting.

"You may touch my foot," she said calmly, "with your lips."

He looked uncomfortable. He cleared his throat.

She extended her leg and foot, and lifted it. She waited. They looked at one another for a few moments.

He cupped her heel in his palm. He lifted her foot and lowered his head. He kissed her arch, his lips pressing warmly and at length. Abruptly she yanked her foot free.

She sat with arms folded across her breast and looking coolly at him she began to grin slowly, derisively.

He turned so red his face looked bursting. He came

upright with a roar. He seized her ankles, forced them apart, and pulled her whole body halfway down the chaise. He inserted himself roughly between her spread thighs.

He fumbled with one hand trying to open his trousers and attempted to hold her down with the other.

Seething with fury, Nikki delivered a lightning fast series of kicks and fist blows, her body arching, twisting, heaving. When he got his hand near her face she snapped, fastening her teeth into the flesh at the outer edge of his palm. She drew blood. He tried to jerk away and she hung on, continuing to roll and heave her body and kick and punch at him. He had to use his other hand to pinion one of her arms. As his body shifted, she rolled out from under, only then releasing his bloody hand.

She flew across to the door, opened it and stood there panting, watching him get up.

"Come on," she said impatiently. "Get yourself together and get out of here right now."

He came across the room, face averted, his taste for erotics considerably diminished.

He paused. "I'm sorry I done that. I promise I won't never do nothing like that again. Don't call the law on me."

"Thanks to your natural incompetence there's nothing to call them about, you clumsy oaf. Get out!"

She slammed the door at his back, then stood with her head tilted haughtily, a triumphant grin on her face.

Ten seconds later she began to tremble all over and cry like a baby.

Chapter Four

     Her makeup and hair-do were ruined and she needed time to recompose herself and abolish that ugliness before she went to Vic. By the time she was dressed and on the way to his office, she was a half-hour late.

Nikki had been "promised" to Vic Hollister the day she was born, when he was four. Through her childhood there had been a running joke, nonetheless expressing the serious hopes of their fathers, that she and Vic were going to marry some day. Until she was seven she believed absolutely that she was his girl. In fact, as docile, sweet Nicolette, in contrast to the defiant, rebellious Nikki she became in her early teens, she had believed everything she was told.

She had been, as her mother unhappily remembered, "such a rewarding child: pretty and smiling and obedient and loving." She'd been her mother's girl, her daddy being at the time a treat for special occasions, wonderful but remote, as from another world. Vic was from another world, too, for he was male, and Nicolette, always the special pet of some older girl, was a girls' girl, and the least naughty—or most prissy—among them.

Boys weren't dainty and clean but mean and rough. During riding lessons they'd flick their whips at the seat of her jodhpurs or nudge her little derby forward over her eyes. At dancing class or indoor parties, they wouldn't behave nicely, but teased, tried to muss her dress, pulled her hair, said improper words.

It was Nicolette's understanding that if they got the chance they'd pull her dress up, her panties down, put her on her back and lay on top of her just because boys liked to get girls' clothes dirty and hurt them.

Vic wasn't terrible like that. She assumed he felt loving toward her like everybody was supposed to, and she didn't doubt he was as proud and happy that she was his girl as her daddy was. Other boys said if she'd be their girl they wouldn't pull her hair and they gave her candy. She ate it, thanked them and, like a proper little lady, gave them permission to bring future gifts. But, she explained, she had to be Vic's girl.

The reason she had to be Vic's girl was because she was Vic's girl. Simple. She didn't have to think any more about it than she did about breathing, or the fact that she and her parents all happened to be in the same family. She felt that being Vic's girl was part of the natural order of things, which was obviously as unchangeable as it was good.

Her father liked Vic, calling him a bright, manly little

chap and praising his horsemanship and way of handling hunting dogs and guns. Her mother was impressed by his politeness and good looks, and the fact he came from "good stock," the son of a gentleman and scholar, Judge Hollister. Vic had been a sturdy, rather chunky boy with dark hair and nice brown eyes. There'd been a serious, almost adult tone about his wide, handsome face, though when he grinned he had dimples and looked like a frisky, healthy baby. He was so nice to look at and so solid that she liked to be around him.

Still, he was an odd sort of beau. He wouldn't hug or kiss her. If she managed to get on his lap, he put her off. Whichever family was visiting the other, Vic's idea of fun was to go out to the stable, saddle a horse and take off—alone. Occasionally he got away without her, but before long she'd be mounted and in pursuit, yelling his name and getting no answer. If she caught him—often he just vanished—she'd give him a bright-beaming, self-satisfied smile as if she were the good fairy who'd just granted his dearest wish. Vic would laugh so hard he'd almost fall off his horse.

She complimented and praised him a lot, thinking he was too manly and shy to say nice things without prompting. He didn't take the hints. However sweetly she looked at him he just stayed aloof, sometimes grinning slightly. Or he might reach down and pat her shoulder. He did that once when she was five and he was nearly ten, and she said admiringly, "My goodness, Victor, you're so tall! And strong, too. I bet you could pick me up easy."

"You know I'm not going to fall for a trick like that, Nicolette."

"You act like you'd break me. Is that because you think I'm a doll? I bet you do think that's what I am, a pretty doll, don't you?"

"That's it. And boys don't play with dolls," he said, smiling down indulgently at her. "That make everything clear to you?"

She looked at him suspiciously. "I don't know why you even come over to see me."

"Because my mother twists my ear."

"All right for you!" she cried. She gazed at him unhappily, pushing out her underlip.

"Now look at you getting your feelings hurt. I was just spoofing."

"Honest?"

"Sure," he said, his nice eyes gentle on her. "You know how your daddy and mine both spoof you. I do, too. See? That's all. Don't feel bad."

She was immediately sunny. "Let's kiss and make up."

"We haven't been mad. Just spoofing. You take spoofs too seriously sometimes, Nicolette. Like our folks saying we'll get married."

"Why, we will! People have to get married when they grow up; everybody knows that."

"No they don't. There's no law. I'm going to be a lawyer so I ought to know. And even if there was, I wouldn't have to marry *you*."

"I'm going to tell my mother on you!"

"I tell you what let's do," he laughed. "Let's talk it over in about twenty years."

In about three years they did. She wasn't quite nine, he was thirteen. She was much taller, but stripe thin and Vic had not only shot up considerably and filled out, but had begun to shave. The disparity in their ages and size was more pronounced than ever. He had begun to have dates—with girls with breasts, as she knew. He was getting so far out of reach it was nearly hopeless.

One Friday afternoon she saw him in town with some boys his age. She yelled and ran to him in a state of excitement. But when she got there, she knew how skimpy she was and she was aware of the annoyed attitude of his friends and was so afraid he'd be irritated that she became tongue-tied and trembled all over. Although her body was nothing, her face was as striking then as now and she forced all his attention to it, gazing at him compellingly, her luminous green eyes eloquent.

"You wanted to talk to me, Nicolette?" he said soothingly.

She nodded, smiling nervously at the others. He told them, "Excuse me. I think this's private. I'll see you around."

"What I was going to say," she began, and broke off as they walked away. "I guess nothing."

"It wasn't 'nothing.' You're all worked up. We'll go over and have a soda, all right?"

"No, that would be like a date. I already know you don't want to be in public with me. It's beneath your dignity. I was going to ask you to come to my dancing school party next week, because this time we can invite outsiders. I wanted you to be my date and . . ." She felt her eyes brim and she swallowed. ". . . I was going to blurt it out. Then I couldn't shame you in front of those boys. I *know* you wouldn't come any more than you'd ever come to my birthday parties with those little kids." She stopped against a building wall and looked at him. "Would you?"

"You answered it yourself," Vic said. "It's impossible. You're just too young. I wish you would get over this crush you've got on me! Will you *try*?"

"I try. I'm not boy-crazy. I don't think about boys at all, because they're nothing. They're insignificant and trivial, and I'm too smart for them. You're the only boy I can look up to, Vic. I'm not interested in having real dates with necking and all, and I wouldn't be allowed to even if I was. So I'll just do like you want and wait till I'm old enough. Then we'll be in love."

"Nicolette, I don't want you to count on any such thing! I'm talking straight. I'm saying the truth and I want you to hear it. Understand? You and I are friends. We always will be. You can count on that. But it's never going to be a romantic thing."

Nikki didn't know how she'd reacted. Had she smiled, told him she understood and that if he couldn't be bothered with her she couldn't with him either, and then strolled away with an indifferent "So long, Vic"? The scene had always blurred in her memory. Now, reaching the county seat fifteen minutes late for her appointment, she knew she wouldn't have called him "Vic" but "Victor" in those days.

There was no parking space near Vic's office in the Hollister Building opposite the front of the courthouse. The first opening she found was in the block behind the courthouse. She angled into the curb, got out and fed the meter, her gaze averted from the wall area beside Beckwith's Hardware. That was the very wall she'd had her back against while Vic was making things so unmistakably clear she couldn't, as hard as she tried, misunderstand. Whether or not she remembered exactly, she knew she hadn't accepted the situation sensibly or shown the slightest self-respect.

Her features tightened. She turned and walked with a short, quick, unflowing stride across the square, heading for the Hollister Building. That's where she—or rather that sickening, spineless child Nicolette—had headed then. To her daddy and Judge Hollister. She had dragged along, feeling abandoned, her shoulders weighted, eyes downcast, her face miserable.

Probably she had been fully aware of the people in the square and played the tragic, broken little figure to the dramatic hilt. Nikki grinned tartly. An instant later she sobered. Trying to substitute cuteness for genuine, heartfelt emotion just because it embarrassed her was to counterfeit and degrade true feeling.

What on earth was she ashamed of about that long-ago situation? Certainly not her capacity to feel things intensely; that was, and she hoped always would be, a part of her very fiber. She shrugged nervously. No, she didn't so much deny the feelings involved. What she was trying to change was her role. It was less disturbing to imagine she had maintained some control over the situation, that she'd been, at least partly, an actress swaying an audience, and thus not helpless at all.

For many years they'd had almost no contacts, Vic going off to military school, then college. Those summers he was home she was often traveling with her parents. Vic wasn't in the picture when, at thirteen, she made the drastic transition from Nicolette to Nikki.

He'd have scarcely recognized the new person. As her father had said, her birth as a young woman was like a crocodile coming out of the egg snapping at the world. Simultaneously with the thrust of her new breasts, her sharp mind began to slash out of the phony pink-cocoon world in which she'd been reared. She scoffed at the fraudulence of the very word "gentleman," despised hypocrisy, scorned to be "a pretty, passive pleasing nothingness of a lady; because that's the same as a whore!"

Her sexual emergence was feverish. She became bristlingly aware of the intentions of every male, while girls who'd been friends became bristlingly aware of her as a rival. Even—*especially*—her mother had felt the rivalry. Then the defeat as she was shunted to the sidelines while Nikki and her father became more and more absorbed with each other.

The intense, prolonged battle Nikki and her father had engaged in and which, finally she had won, destroying him, centered on those spankings. Nikki would goad him with an insolence, or disobedience, providing the excuse. Then there would be the breathlessly exciting walk to his office on the first floor or up to his third-floor den. The door would shut and they would be alone. There would be that glittering feel of his anger and mastery, that honed look about his lean, tall body and devilishly handsome face.

She would be thrown down across his knee, her upturned bottom stripped bare, her soft thighs locked tightly between his hard, sinewy legs. It was degrading. It violated her dignity and femininity to be forced into that indelicate, exposed position, to have her rights abolished by superior physical force.

She would struggle, demand release or plead; sometimes she gave way helplessly to tears of rage and frustration and beat the floor with her fists. And yet . . . yet . . . knowing that what was coming was inevitable, she would feel a sort of tingling, shamelessly pleasant undercurrent of anticipation. Then it would begin, his hand coming down in a rush of hard cracking blows that stung and burned her naked flesh. And soon . . . soon . . . insidiously mingling with her angry resentment and pain she would feel tiny stabbings and spasms, sensation that burst into wild sexual pleasure. More than once, twisting her head around abruptly, she caught the lusting, trancelike look of guilty enjoyment on his face.

After each session he would come to her room, tender and contrite, and promise a gift or grant a new privilege or withdraw some rule she'd been required to obey. And bit by bit, as time went by, he surrendered his authority, yielded his power to her. He'd made his first concession after a spanking because she had felt crushed and he'd been overcome by remorse and tenderness. Some of that element remained, but more and more, on later occasions, guilt dominated him.

Nikki had exploited it, and exulting in power, she'd

changed the world around her. Notably, she'd had him sell all their gentlemanly gaited show horses in favor of professional athletes in the form of a racing stable. What's more, they'd won big stakes at Belmont, Aqueduct and Bowie.

She'd loved her power and pushed for more and more. She had wanted to push so damned hard that he would rise up in magnificent wrath to his true height and reassert himself grandly. He kept retreating and drinking more and more, and becoming weaker. She'd wanted him to be strong and put her down and be above her where he belonged. In fact, though she hadn't known it consciously then, she'd literally wanted him to get on top of her.

Sex aside, she had wanted him to be stronger because she needed that strength for protection. He'd been a tower, unassailable; she hadn't really imagined she could weaken it and bring it down. It had shaken her confidence deeply, she now knew, and her necessity to test men sprang from that experience.

She resolved to be her own strength, independent of outside protection. Knowledge was power, she knew, education the road to it and her mind the vehicle. Precocious, she finished high school at fourteen and demanded to go to college at once. Her parents closed ranks against her and enforced a year's delay. She locked herself in her rooms and read encyclopedically every day and frequently half the night, since she needed only four or five hours sleep.

Her satisfaction in progressing mentally wasn't enough, she had to rub it in. She told them—especially *him*—she was learning seven times as much as she would have in school and that the forces trying, under the guise of love, to hold her mind down to the level of a child—or a *lady*—might win a battle, but never the war against her.

When she began seeing Vic regularly again, she was seventeen and had completed two years of college. Her grasp and range of ideas convinced him she had a mind, and her academic record, presently to earn her a Phi Beta Kappa key, impressed him. It was marvelous to have such an ally, and she let Vic know she appreciated him.

They didn't have dates so much as exhilarating talk fests that roamed freely through a world of ideas, philosophies, theories, speculations. They had stimulating, informal debates for the sheer pleasure of contests and the enjoyment of each other's arguments. Not infrequently they switched sides somewhere along the line and ended up defending the position they'd been attacking.

Vic knew more and was not only tougher-minded but a master of formal logic, where she couldn't hold her own—unless he "carried" her. In other areas she could run circles around him—unless she slowed up. They strove for a certain type of ideal relationship that depended on their meeting as near-equals. And since there couldn't be victory without defeat, they both backed off if they were getting the other in trouble. They looked on each other as refreshing companions, then as really good friends.

They shared a reluctance to tamper with things by introducing a romantic, sexual, possibly emotionally disruptive element. He played a field of local girls and she, too, had occasional party-type dates while home on vacations. They often met with other partners at a dance, club affair or house party, and usually there was no friction. But if it should happen that a general group discussion got under way, the social amenities of loyalty to the partner of the evening vanished. Automatically they rallied to each other's cause, even if privately they'd fought on the same issue.

It couldn't be said they were so platonic that they were indifferent to the other one's date. Vic began to seem serious about a girl with a vague, dreamlike beauty who spoke in silences, rarely opening her mouth.

Males being inclined to read depth and wisdom into such types, Nikki had a short conversation with her and discovered the secret of her silence. Then, in Vic's presence, Nikki enticed her into stating her views on life, love and things in general. And from the lovely's mouth there poured out a whole dictionary of vapid clichés and banalities.

Next day Vic jumped on her.

"Nikki, what you did to her was beneath you, because she's no match for you."

"Must you talk like a *gentleman*? You say Miss Stupidity Unlimited is no match for me, so I shouldn't have tripped her up. False reasoning. It assumes that because she's a kind of cripple she's harmless. Not so. She's attractive. A man could build up enough sexual steam to wilt his wits. By the time he found out what she was, it wouldn't seem to matter. He might even marry her and ruin his life. If I nipped that possibility, I did what a friend should to protect a friend. And my motives were no more than ninety percent selfish. I'm proud of me."

He gave her a jeering, but affectionate grin. "Not that it was exactly marriage I had in mind."

"Well, if all you had in mind was going to bed with her, why jump on me? I didn't do her any harm as a sex prize. Am I to understand, Victor, that when you take a girl in a bedroom you sit her down, administer an intelligence test and if she doesn't pass you withhold stud service?"

"That's good. Very good." He laughed. "But we've never told each other jokes like that. Let's not start."

"All right."

"You sound moody."

"Do I? Sorry. Actually I couldn't agree with you more that we should block out sex. We've got a unique friendship and I wouldn't want it turned into something commonplace."

"Now, about your argument the other afternoon that the theories of Romantics, Rationalists and Idealists were, essentially, only different costumes designed to hide the same truths," he said, steering them easily into another gripping, but impersonal exchange.

It wasn't only with her that Vic seemed to stand above personal involvement. She sometimes wondered whether he had any private ego at all. In the company of other law students and, later, young lawyers, she'd seen him get wrought up about some principle or other but take no offense at what she'd have considered personal insult. Partly this was because even in boyhood he'd thought of himself as belonging to the world of law. It was an article of faith with him that this was a nation of laws, not men, and he believed with conviction that passions were the enemies of justice.

She needled delicately: "It's true we'd drop back into anarchy and the world would be a murderous jungle without laws. And men of principle protect our freedoms, but nobody as unemotional as you could get elected to office."

"Possibly true," he said stiffly. "If they're looking for a sequin-toothed smiling charmer, I'm not their boy."

"I did it! Got under your skin. What a day!" she said gleefully. Then she was sorry. "Vic, I didn't mean it. Honestly, I respect and admire you so much. It's only —oh, nothing. I'm embarrassed. I might offend you—no, not that exactly—it might sound as if I don't like you. Promise not to take it that way?"

"Oh, good Lord, such squirming, Nikki! Go right ahead."

"Well, I was disappointed in your boxing exhibition I went up to see last spring. There you were, the holder of the intercollegiate light heavyweight title, the champion, but you powder-puffed that palooka all the way through."

"It was a charity show and all the bouts were exhibitions, not fights. You know that."

"I went there excited, wanting to see you in action, winning. I wanted to cheer and I was sitting there all set to beat blisters on my hands and scream my head off for you, Vic. But it wasn't a real fight."

"It was a demonstration of first-rate skill appreciated by experts. I made a monkey out of him."

"It would have been more exciting if—"

"Hell hath no fury like a noncombatant. If there'd been any point in it, I could have made a bloody mess and knocked him out."

"I wouldn't really have liked that. What I wanted, I guess, was . . . well . . . to see if you were capable of getting fighting mad. It gives a man a thrilling tone and would make you handsomer and manlier-looking than ever." Just talking about it made her bright-eyed and slightly breathless.

"Damned if that's not a hell of a note! Getting excited by the brutal part of a man, liking the look of him when he's at his mean-tempered worst!"

She gazed fascinatedly at him. She said huskily, "You're looking mean-tempered handsome *right now*!"

He walked away, came back and looked at her with such disgust she cringed.

A moment later she said slashingly, "What's so horrible about wanting a man with some fight in him? It's the anger and meanness and intensity, or to put it another way, the alive human nature that you find most attractive about *me*, too. I can prove it! Remember your saying it was astonishing that I'd turned out such a beauty? What did I say?"

"What did you say? Why, that you'd always been very pretty but I'd been too high and mighty to notice."

"You said you'd noticed all right. That I'd certainly been a pretty enough girl, but dull. By dull, you meant *nice*. It takes bitchiness to attract men, maybe because they're dull louts who can't feel anything weaker than an explosion."

"You're an explosion all right." He laughed, enjoying her. "But hardly an authority on men. I didn't mean you were dull because you were sexless. You had such a nice, conformist little mind. It accepted; it didn't question; it didn't, in a word, *think*. That's the big change in you that makes you stimulating, Nicolette."

"Don't 'Nicolette' me! I know some ugly men who think better than I do. So they should stimulate you more," she jeered.

"You don't think a man can be around you without lusting. A typical neo-Victorian virgin's attitude. An overvaluation of the unruptured hymen, based on—"

"I know! I know! Property values, et cetera, et cetera. But don't accuse *me* of thinking in terms of having a commodity for sale, with marriage the price."

"Also characteristic of the modern neo-Victorian virgin is a great academic knowledge of sex."

"I suppose you could say mine's an academic knowledge, since the three men I've slept with so far were in college."

"You're kidding!" He laughed. "You *are* kidding."

"I am not. I'm sure this is offensive to the neo-puritan-cum-Victorian male, and marks me down as a soiled lily on the pond of life, h'm?"

"No. Even if I believed you."

"I read faces in my spare time. Let's face it, Vic. If true, I've proven myself no proper lady, and no priggish proper Virginia gentleman will tolerate that in his womenfolk."

"You're wrong that I'd take that attitude. Nonetheless, I know you're too fine a person to have let—"

"There are exactly 2,739,260 people in insane asylums who were too fine for sex, at least in its more standard forms."

"Exactly 2,739,206?" He laughed uneasily. "Nikki! You're not foolin'?"

The pleading note in his voice made her look at him sharply. All his impersonality was gone. His features were soft, as if an invisible glaze that usually held them firm had dissolved. They were outdoors, on her land. They'd had an invigorating tramp through the woods, along the creek and up and down waves of rolling land that bright, cold January afternoon. For the past twenty minutes they'd been on a long, broad level ridge top a quarter-mile from the main house and at an elevation providing an expansive view of the open country. It was a man's setting and Vic fit it ruggedly, looking virile in his thick walking shoes, gray pants and short, dark-blue coat open over a black turtleneck sweater.

Till this moment it had been a good, clean fight, maybe just an exhibition, with no chance of anyone's getting hurt. Now there was an anxious, pained, expression in his fine brown eyes. She turned away uncomfortably.

"Well?" Vic said.

"*Must* I admit something? Either lying or the other?" she said peevishly. "I'd think you'd lay off when you've got me cornered. After all, I'm a girl."

He didn't answer, just looked away, a frown across his protruding brow ridge. He was tall, with good shoulders, broad-based neck and well-set head. Hatless, his thick short hair and precisely cut sideburns showed darkly against his fair skin. His clean-lined jaw and the strong male sculpturing of his forehead and cheekbones were formidable, but he was vulnerable. Surprisingly. It distressed her. His gaze followed an old green car on a brown dirt road in the distance for a while, shifted to a man walking with an Irish setter on a hill.

Still not looking at Nikki, he said, "I understand what your answer is. And it's all right."

He turned with a strained smile. He gazed at her with such melting tenderness that she suddenly began to scrape her underlip. She thought she was going to cry. But she scowled and said nastily, "Oh, it's all right, is it? And don't give me that wounded, forgiving look. I'm not ashamed. Except of you. Because you're hurt about it. Because you're weak enough to let it hurt you. Some man!"

Dull red color suffused his face. The cords of his neck stood out; the arteries flanking his windpipe became visible, pulsing heavily. He glared, and under the threat of his narrowed eyes, her eyes opened wider, the green irises showing round and brilliant against expanses of clear white.

In that moment he was dangerous. Unpredictable. She felt the atmosphere of violence he projected. Urgent flight impulses raced along the nerves of her fleet young legs and her toes twitched faintly. But she didn't move. She blinked her eyes once and waited, alert.

"Let's walk," he said, snapping the tension. He gripped her arm, turned her and started toward the house. "It's time we got back. It's because you've got a special place in my life that you've got the special privilege to talk to me like that. Even when you know I can't to you."

"The reason you don't hit back is to make me feel guilty!"

"Do you?"

"No."

"You attacked me because I showed concern about what happened to you, and you're not ashamed of yourself?"

"I *won't* be. You acted like my having lovers had been a disease instead of the healthy, instinctive thing to do. In theory, you know as well as I do that the whole sexual code is based on a damned lie. It says girls in their teens, obviously meant for and ready for procreation, have no sex! Or if they do, they're somehow evil. The whole drive to deny simple, wholesome truth or to distort its meaning with flossy romantic sentimentality, is a violation if not a perversion of nature. If you feel and know the plain, clean facts of your own nature, they try to twist it around and make you feel ashamed and guilty. And if you not only feel and know but act, daring to be free instead of imprisoning yourself with rules you don't believe in, then even your best friend cringes away—or 'forgives' you."

"You know quite well, Nikki, there are other serious factors involved in those codes and laws. If you could abolish them tomorrow, you wouldn't."

"I didn't say I would. I'm not out to live other people's lives. Just mine. And mine I'll live according to *my* rules. As much as I can get by with it—which is plenty. That's how I feel, Vic, and that's how I am, and if I can't be honest about it with you—well, I hope I can, because I'll say this, I think more of you than I ever did of any other man."

"Including the unholy three?"

"I didn't care a whit for any of them. Compared to how I felt—and feel—about you, they didn't *exist*."

"Then how could you give yourself in the most personal intimate relationship? I'm assuming you had this sex drive which you were wholesomely and instinctively obedient to, so you weren't frigid."

"Vic, you're a musty traditionalist. Yes, I liked the sex part, but Shakespeare notwithstanding, love's not a woman's whole existence. When it was done, it was done; I was busy with other things. Never even thought of them. Out of sight, out of mind. I liked knowing the power I had over them; they had none over me."

"Well, Nikki, I can't understand it. Maybe in the emotional area I am a musty traditionalist. However, I'm up-to-date enough in my thinking to ask you to go to bed with me."

"I'd rather not. No, I don't mean that. I'd really like to. But . . . I don't know. Please don't ask me."

"I am asking. You're exciting. I'd love to go to bed with you."

"I'm scared."

"That's the most exasperating damned answer I ever heard. Scared. Of *me?*"

"Yes. No. I mean . . . scared it wouldn't work out."

"I take it I don't rouse you *that* way," he said, bitterly.

"That's a laugh!" She laughed.

"Then by God you're *going* to sleep with me. *Tonight!*"

"Well, by God, I'm *not* going to sleep with you . . . Vic." She pulled at his sleeve, stopping him. When he looked at her, she said gently, "Vic, I'm sorry. Really I am. But you're not like anybody else. With you it would be too important. Do try to understand. I just couldn't risk it.

"Vic, I want you to know something. Those three are past tense. Since you and I've been close the way we have, there hasn't been anybody else. So you needn't start thinking back over our friendship and getting bitter, imagining I was making some kind of fool of you. Hear?"

Presently they walked on to the house.

The next time they walked that path together it was late June. One week before, she had received her college diploma and the same day had had the pleasure of seeing Dolores, her long-time roommate and dearest friend, happily married.

Nikki had wanted her parents to be there during her final days on campus, and they had come. She'd wanted to end the years of submerged conflicts when they'd lived, semi-alienated, in a state of truce with her. They had all tried to act as if there'd been no weakening in the flow of love from either side. They hadn't succeeded very well.

The weather was balmy as she approached the house with Vic. Trees and grasses flourished, flowers in the formal gardens burst with color, the very earth surged with life, and she hated the sight of it. She hated herself. Merely to walk was tiring. She had wanted to come outside. Now she wanted only to reach the house and shut herself in and close the blinds and sink down and sleep . . . sleep . . . sleep, a black empty endless sleep.

For they were dead. Suddenly, violently dead, six days ago, in the same plane crash.

The funeral had been three days ago. The burial. The finality of their burial hit her like shock. Double. Her father dead. Her mother dead. They were gone, *Forever!*

She hadn't slept since for more than ten minutes at a time. She looked like hell, she felt like hell. She couldn't bear to be around anyone, not even Vic. He had relieved her of many details and kept in close sympathetic touch. She appreciated his feeling, but she did not want his sympathy. And he wasn't obtrusive. He suggested, but didn't insist, that she let a doctor come and give her some relief.

"I won't have it softened. I won't be drugged. It's not supposed to be comfortable and easy."

"I understand."

"You saw what I did when your daddy was reading the will. I heard those expressions—'my only child' and 'beloved daughter' and sobbed, trying to get rid of the pain that way. I cut their hearts out! I wasn't what they wanted me to be. I became somebody who—"

He cut in: "If you had to go against them to become your own person, that was inevitable, not intentional 'cutting their hearts out.'"

"You mustn't make excuses for me. What I'm going through is raw and true. And I'm going to endure it, the way it is. Please don't try to take the edge off of it. Just leave me alone."

"I'll go. But I'll be checking back."

She didn't argue. But as soon as possible after he left she got into a car and took flight. She had no goal in mind. But she knew that more than anything in the world she craved to lean on him.

She got to Richmond, vaguely planning to go to an aunt's where a homelike security was readily available. But she went to the airport. She chose to fly to Boston only because she couldn't think of anyone she knew there. From Boston she wired Judge Hollister for money and when it came she took off for Los Angeles. Then almost at once she went to Las Vegas. Within an hour of checking in at a hotel, Vic, in person, found her.

She was startled that he had read her mind when she herself hadn't known where she might go. He coaxed her back home, and for two weeks she stayed. Just long enough to discover that he was in love with her. She thought she was in love with him, but she wanted to wait and be sure. An invitation to play in a tennis tournament reached her and she traveled to Chicago. Fortunately or not, she won the tournament.

Sports wasn't her idea of a career, but it had its rewards and soon she was wrapped up in it. For a few months Vic appeared every time she was playing anywhere near home. He became more and more ardent.

Somehow she was afraid that in the emotional area he wouldn't be an unassailable tower of strength. His will might, in that relationship, yield to hers. She wanted to test him, but even more, she wanted to protect him. From her. From her destructiveness. No, he was too fine a man for that. She cared too much for him to take the chance.

Vic finally quit. Their lives separated completely. They never saw each other. They rarely even included a personal note in their business letters.

When Nikki came back home to bring her property to life, one of her happiest prospects was seeing Vic again. She thought she might marry him. At the very least she would have a marvelous affair with him.

However, Vic had taken a wife. A bitch. A rotten bitch who was destroying him.

Chapter Five

Nikki reached the private, mid-block stairway entrance that led to the Hollister law offices in the block-long, two-story Hollister Building. She glanced up and stopped, anger catching her like a claw.

A creature whose hair and eye color was like an enemy's caricature of her own, was coming down the stairs. It was the brassy, red-haired knife-faced, scrawny-chested pseudo-female Vic had married. She wore a raucous-parrot colored green and yellow dress that showed her bony knees; her spike heels sounded as if they would punch through the old boards on the next step. Her hair was puffed out on each side like flamboyant pillows, calculated to excite the male eye and blind it to the sharpness of her narrow face. The woman might be pretty, Nikki thought grudgingly, but amended it, because the prettiness had, like her voice, a harsh quality.

Her name was Evelyn, and on the few occasions

Nikki had been around her she'd observed something so similar to herself that it made her cringe. An aggressive tone about her personality and manner. It was general, not just directed at her. Of course it was possible that her own presence brought out the worst. Nonetheless, Nikki went to great pains to reassure herself that their personalities were only superficially the same.

Though she was challenging and argumentative because she had strong beliefs, she had reasons for them and didn't express herself merely to be unpleasant or shut someone else up.

From a distant booth she'd seen Evelyn at a roundtable restaurant party one night. She remained surly, refusing all efforts to draw her in. She ordered drink after drink and stared defiantly at Vic whenever he noticed she had a new one. At one point Evelyn sat watching a couple across the table discussing something animatedly.

She yelled, "Whattaya talkin' about? Whyncha cut the crap and drink your goddamn drinks? How about that?" She'd laughed, looking around the table, pleased with herself.

At a local horse show, from three boxes away Nikki heard Evelyn say to Vic, "Yah yah yah . . . shut up!" Minutes later he'd fairly dragged her out of the arena, to Nikki's delight. She hoped he'd beat her up when he got her home.

But he couldn't always be around to control her. Only half his law practice was local; he spent time regularly in Richmond and Norfolk, while Evelyn stayed home and disgraced him. Nikki understood the unreliability of rumors from her own experience and she tried to ignore those about Evelyn. But it was whispered she was making a cuckold of Vic.

She'd hardly dared ask Vic why he had married her; the marriage was never mentioned between them. She knew he'd met her while at a convention in Atlanta and that she came from a "good family" in that city. From these skimpy facts Nikki had entirely reconstructed the romance. It might be fantasy, but it was her fantasy and went as she wanted it to. First he'd mistaken her for Nikki. The husband hunter had cunningly made herself seem just what he wanted. She'd seduced him. Next she sobbed that she was pregnant and rushed him to the altar.

His mistake was in not sensing she was fake and also frigid. Also his eye should have told him she was biologically barren and couldn't possibly get pregnant. His final stupidity was being the gentleman. But he couldn't help that any more than she could help sympathizing with him, no matter how angrily she told herself he didn't deserve it.

Evelyn reached the bottom of the stairs as Nikki started up. Passing one another they looked at each other, exchanging one word, "Hello," while their eyes said eloquently, "How I hate you, you bitch!"

On the upswing between the sixth and fifth steps from the top she saw Vic's Aunt Willa, a fixture in the firm for thirty years, facing her from the desk in the big waiting room. Nikki lifted her brows, asking about Vic's mood. Aunt Willa drew the corners of her mouth down, then turned and called, "Vic . . . Nikki's here."

Vic was standing moodily in the dorway of his office when Nikki entered the waiting room. Aunt Willa beamed and called, "C'mon along over here, Sugar 'n' Spice, and give me a hug."

Nikki grinned and obeyed, then completed the lifelong ritual by turning around to be admired. Vic, watching to prevent Aunt Willa whispering confidences about his marriage, nodded at Nikki.

"Hello, Nikki. I'm a little pressed for time."

"How are you, Vic? Coming right away—'Bye, Aunt Willa . . . Sorry I'm late. But I had the orchard demonstration and the breakfast. People wanted to look the place over," she said, moving into the front office, now occupied by "the young judge," since his father's retirement, "and it turned out lots of them stayed for lunch and some will still be there for dinner. I couldn't get away."

She seated herself in one of the heavy armchairs facing his desk while he closed the door and crossed the room. He seated himself—listlessly, she noted unhappily—in the big leather swivel chair whose back was several inches higher than the top of his head.

"I saw you hurrying across the square, so you were trying. And I must say you look splendid."

"That's nice of you," she said, glancing down at herself. She'd dressed to please, not excite. Her makeup was unaccented, her white felt hat covered most of her hair, the linen suit was loose, straight-lined, her gloves, purse, pumps, neat. "Have you been getting in your sunrise rides?"

"Usually, yes. I try to keep fit. I'm on the go a lot and it tires me. Guess I don't have your energy."

"I run down, too," she assured him. He knew she realized he didn't travel excessively and that the work load he carried was something he relished and couldn't account for the fatigue of his spirit. What did account for it was unmentionable between them.

"That breakfast must have cost you a couple of hundred dollars," he said, sitting forward and squinting at a sheet of figures on his desk.

She sighed. "So we're down to business. And that's just what the breakfast was—a business investment. Several hundred years of agricultural experience were represented among my guests. I brain-picked them and did learn and will in the future learn many things."

He held up a hand. "Good rationalization. I'll ask your tax accountant what he thinks. Whatever he thinks, you're already overinvested. I've told you, Nikki, and I've told you. You can't keep pouring it out. You'll have to get it pouring back in. Wait a while. Mark time. Take it easy."

"This is easy for a person of your temperament to say. I'm not built that way."

"You can't do everything at once!"

"You can try," she said tartly.

"You can listen!" he said sharply. "You live like a sybarite. Personal maid. Luxury apartment in New York. Fly to Paris and back like strolling to the drugstore."

"I haven't set foot out of the country for months . . . because the mood hasn't hit me."

He gazed at her with an odd blend of exasperation and tenderness and said softly, "Don't fight me, Nikki. Listen to me. You can afford to be a sybarite. You can also afford to live the other life, running that property. You've done a great job there, Nikki, a sound investment in the future. But a damned heavy investment.

At this time an overinvestment. Still and all, you can afford to be an overinvestor and a sybarite. But you cannot afford to be an overinvestor and a sybarite *and* a big-time Broadway gambler!"

"Vic, must we go over it again and again? What's the point in saying I shouldn't back that play when I've already done it? It's past. I couldn't get it back if I wanted to. And I don't because the play'll be a smash and the best investment I ever made."

"Let's face why you really did that stupid thing. To fool around with that no-talent, big-name, sequin toothed Hollywood glamour boy you hired to be the star," he said with unusual venom. He turned his chair, got up abruptly, went to the window and adjusted the Venetian blind. "That's not my business!" he said coldly.

She sat tensely, looking down at her lap, afraid to look at him after that unexpected flare of naked jealousy. The yearning she'd sometimes seen or imagined in his eyes recently was real, as real as hers for him.

He sat down again, and began to speak calmly.

"Mostly I think you're stage-struck. You were always fooling around in kid plays, and you were hot about your college drama club, I remember. I'm afraid that the subjective element . . ."

He broke off. She was sitting with lowered lids, and she sensed that he was looking at her. She raised her eyes to his, and for a moment of anguish she saw the way he was looking at her. Both averted their eyes, but the thing had been said. And the truth was he not only wanted her but needed her.

She felt a sensation over the skin of her upper back . . . a thrill . . . a chill . . . and remembered Dolores. Her head ached. Dolores had been her best friend and had taken her with love into the warmth of her happy family. And her husband had wanted Nikki and she him and they had been lovers. She had almost destroyed that marriage and she had irrevocably lost her friend and one of the finest relationships of her life. Never, *never*, again, would she risk breaking a marriage—*any* marriage. No matter what she thought of it.

"The subjective element of why I do anything is out of my lawyer's province," she said tightly.

"Not when it threatens your whole survival. Not by

a damned sight, Nikki. You've got big loans to repay. You've had to sell off a basketful of blue chip securities. You've got in deeper and deeper to the point where *everything* has to pay off. Luck's got to be running your way on every throw. One really rough spell of unusual weather—too much rain or a drought—and some of the crops you're counting on will be ruined! You think about that, Nikki."

"Well, what I think is you can't win if you don't play. The fault, my dear Victor," she snapped, "is not in taking bold, calculated risks. It's in people scared to take them. You've been reading the accounting firm's statement and looking at the brokerage account reports and getting scared. I might call you to account about why it is you're dealing, in my behalf, with brokers who hold onto the kinds of investment that can't make big gains."

"It's the only kind of firm I'll let you deal with. I'm not here to shoot craps with the money your daddy left you, but to protect it. In spite of you!"

His face flushed. His eyes glittered at her. His penetration was like a sexual thrust and she felt waves of excitement. Behind his rage was love, protectiveness. She adored him! And she *must not let herself* feel that strongly!

"I'm sick of your stuffy nobility," she said, angrily getting to her feet. "Don't try to tell me how to live. If I want to throw everything away, I'll throw it away! In case you need any further instructions," she said arrogantly, "you can reach me in New York. I'm flying there later tonight."

"Nobody in the world can talk to me like that!" He stood up, fists clenched and braced on his desk. He was quivering.

Nikki laughed suddenly.

"Aw, Vic," she said, hurrying around the desk to him. "I didn't mean what I said. I appreciate what you're trying to do. I'm sorry the way I talked. Honestly I am. Don't be mad at me."

Gradually he relaxed. He shrugged, curled an arm out around her shoulder and hugged her briefly.

"Oh, well," he said, grinning down at her. "I'll kill you some other time."

"I sure wouldn't blame you."

He lit a cigarette and they stood near each other in a relaxed mood. The high-ceilinged, old-fashioned office with its glass-front bookcases and framed photos and the warm light was familiar and pleasant and it was so sweet just being with him, feeling his presence. She would like to give to him, not necessarily herself, but whatever he might need. This was his feeling for her, too. He cared so much. He was such a good man. Nothing and nobody, including herself, should ever hurt him.

And then the unself-conscious, lovely mood was gone. An auto horn began to blast repeatedly. It was his wife, sitting across the street and scowling up at the office windows.

Chapter Six

Planes crash, she thought, boarding the flight to New York just after dark, *but not this one.* Nonetheless when they were airborne at cruising altitude, she smiled down a little wistfully at the landscape, lit by a descending moon and dotted with white blocks and irregular patches of blossoming apple orchards.

Two other eyes watched the ground, electronic eyes on the underside of the plane, at nose and tail. They were part of the ground-speed indicator system, measuring the time it took the plane to pass over a point of light or darkness below. A triumph of modern technology, the idea was ingenious and it was a testimonial to human intellect and it was stolen from insects, she thought amusedly. For the eyes of a honeybee registered the passage of light and darkness over their multi-thousand lenses and told the tiny flier, among other things, how much headway it was making against the wind.

After dinner, lulled by the engines' drone, she curled up and slept. She dreamed of "honey thunder" in orchard trees and of electronic bees dancing on hive walls.

There was a touch on her shoulder and the bees, along with some sort of brilliant thought, vanished. In the blurred, timeless transition from sleep to wakefulness she saw the blue eyes and blond hair of her dearest friend, Dolores, her lovely face warm and forgiving. Nikki smiled with such pure pleasure that the blond, blue-eyed stewardess' neutral expression gave way spontaneously to a delighted grin.

"My goodness, but you're a happy waker. I hated disturbing you, you looked so peaceful. But we'll be landing in about ten minutes now, so you better tighten up your seat belt."

"Sure, thanks. Yes, I will."

As the stewardess moved away she sat straight, snugged the seat belt around her, glanced at her watch. Swallowing to relieve pressure in her ears, she looked out the window. There was no land or city or sky for they were slicing through a cloud mass. The landing lights were on and the powerful beams pierced the clouds and bent and spread and blazed with sudden whitenesses in a breath-taking rush. The display was so gripping she barely noticed the jolts of turbulence.

But she was aware with a curious, dark excitement that other planes might be out there in that gray chaos. The possibilities, she thought with a tight grin, were as fatal as fate which called for a fatalistic shrug.

Suddenly they were in the clear under a mile-high ceiling. The landing was routine. She left the plane and the moment her feet touched ground the last of an invisible network of chains dropped away. She had a luscious sense of freedom. The aggravations of getting through the terminal to the cabs were stimulating. A rough-and-ready cabbie, eyeing her appreciatively, came forward, reaching for her hand luggage.

"Right this way, Miss Nikki Duquesne!" he said triumphantly.

"You know me?" Her eyes widened in surprise.

He laughed and remarked airily to a fellow driver, "Read it and weep, buddy. Page three. Nikki Duquesne. And Mike Tremont's got her." Handing her into the cab he said, "To the Waldorf and away we go!"

He got in and grinning back at her, handed her a small publication called *Gotham Comings and Goings*.

"How did they know?" she said, half-frowning at her listed name.

"They know everything." He flipped the flag and got rolling. "You're asking how'd I know you by sight. A very interesting question, Miss Duquesne, or if you'd rather, Nikki, and call me Mike. Seen you on TV."

"But I haven't *been* on TV."

"I get off work three mornings ago and step into Pat's Bar—Pat 'n' Mike y'know, near the Garden over on Eighth. They got the color TV. I'm watching the sports part of the 'Dawn' show. The man says, 'We been reading Lennie Lyons and Cholly Knickerbocker and the Night Tattler and all the gossipers about a certain delish dish, Nikki Duquesne, that's seen here and there-about with this French count and that Hollywod movie star and the other zillionaire, and how she's backing Broadway shows and going up and down the line of fancy beaneries and hotsy clubs in her sables and diamonds, everywhere from Uptown to the beat joints in the Village. Only she belongs to the world of sports and the time has come to reclaim her.' So he run this film clip with you with a ribbon in your hair and a shorty white tennis skirt in a game at Forest Hills."

He whistled. "What shots! Tennis *and* camera both. So you win. Till then it's been black and white. Then people are swarming around you, with you laughing it up pretty and talking fast. They change cameras to color real sudden! Wham! it's a full-face shot with them green eyes and that gorgeous fiery hair and I tell you, you like to jumped out of that tube, you came across so good. Punchy! And you talked good. Sharp. Funny. You missed it if you never seen it; I tell you! When'd it happen?"

"Two years ago. I saw it then. You liked me, h'm? That's great. Mike, you're a flattering welcoming committee. And a marvelous surprise."

"A pleasure. I and my buddy spotted you as a standout when you were ankling along among the scruff back there in the terminal. I says right off she's *somebody*. And mine. I claimed you, only he don't allow it unless I can name you before he does. Only right at the last minute did I fully recognize you. He sour-graped he was glad owing to beauties don't tip good. I said, 'Keep abreast. They're different nowadays. They got their public image and the tightwad thing don't do nobody except Jack Benny good.' I had him for a fare three different times and in real life he ain't that way."

"That's how it is with me, Mike. People get the impression I'm free and easy and open-handed, and in real life I'm the opposite," she said, tongue in cheek. He swiveled his head around almost 180 degrees to study her.

Nikki began laughing. "Scared you, didn't I? Well, even if I wasn't a good tipper, you'd be the exception. Just between us, Mike, I'm not going to the Waldorf, but to my own apartment." She gave him the address in the seventies just off Fifth.

"Smart! Steer the public off and leave the Waldorf worry about them while you keep your privacy. Y'see that item in the *Broadway Buzz* column yesterday?"

"No. About me?"

"Not if you say no, Nikki." He turned again and winked. "It merely remarked on a rich girl-about-town with a big dollar and heart stake in a draah-mah who has been secretly rehearsing the top femme lead at her country estate and plans to take off the wraps and dazzle forth as an actress on opening night."

"It may refer to me, but there's nothing to it."

"Smart! Stay under wraps, till you're ready to spring it on 'em. Come on sudden, like that switch to color on TV."

She got him steered away from her finally. He held forth on the UN, traffic, juvenile delinquency, politics, psychiatry, people in general, speaking of the whole city as if it were a wayward child with a hopeless future. Nikki half-listened, nodding. Crossing the bridge there was something intoxicating and aphrodisiacal into Manhattan she looked at the skyline, thinking that about arriving at night.

Mike pulled up at the curb in front of her apartment, got out, came around and opened the door for her as the doorman, Jack Tenn, came strolling out under the marquee in his sky-blue uniform.

"Here she is, buddy," Mike called.

"Well, well, Miss Duquesne; good to see you. I'll take the luggage, driver. What's the fare? I'll take care of it."

"Never mind, buddy. Nikki already settled with me. What you can do for her, though, is take my card. If the occasion should arise in the small hours when she wishes to go out unaccompanied and desires a trustworthy driver, phone me. Best of luck, Nikki. I enjoyed the intelligent discussions. I'll be there for that big opening night surprise." He winked knowingly, went around, got in and drove away.

"Big man!" Jack scoffed and went with her luggage to the door. "Every time I talk to a cop I like cabbies; every time I talk to a cabbie I like cops."

He held the door and she entered the small lobby.

"Any messages?"

"Emissaries from Europe, Hollywood, Broadway. I'm getting rich taking messages to give you. Wait, I'll get the batch of 'em. He went into and came out of a little office off the foyer with a stack of notepaper clipped together. He proceeded to the elevator. She followed slowly, shuffling through the notes. Anton . . . Kris . . . Jean Eveux . . . Greg Thrimble . . . Dave Proller . . .

Jack stood by as she keyed open her thirteenth-floor apartment. He went in with her, made a tour of the rooms, came back.

"It's O. K. When's the maid due?"

"Tomorrow sometime. By train. Jack, I'm still not here yet. I'll phone down later and let you know who I'm expecting." She opened her purse. He shook his head.

"Forget it, this time. G'night. Just let me know who can come up and I'll let him past."

Alone, she took off hat and coat, unpinned her hair, dimmed the lights, opened the broad drapes and looked out over the city with a gleeful little smile. She paced back and forth along the edge of the vast silver-gray carpet, thinking, yes, that's what the city at night was, an aphrodisiac. She opened two casements a few inches, admitting a fresh, slightly moist flow of air and the blur of traffic sounds. It wasn't yet eleven. A perfect carnival of moving colored lights bombarded her senses.

She was ready, overready, for love. Her health demanded it, her senses craved it. Who, she thought, who should she call—or summon—she amended—as lover for the night?

A worshipful animal mass like Truck Wyzowski, her first lover, who'd spread whipped cream on her naked body and licked it off? An aesthetically pleasing mama's boy like Archer Cole whom she'd almost decided to marry in San Francisco in order to settle down near Dolores and Jim Thelton? Or like Jim Thelton, who had been as tender and sympathetic as a father, yet so virile and thrillingly controlled he had forced her to repeated ecstasies before yielding to his own pleasure?

In no case would she want an encounter with a person like John Barket, fundamentally decent and worthwhile but "lacking the winning punch." She frowned. No, he hadn't lacked anything. She had castigated him viciously because of his virtue. Because, moved by her pleas and tears, he *had* withdrawn, had *not* raped her. She didn't want anything so emotionally demanding.

Nor in fact did she want anything but sensation. Once, just once, she would like to experience the sexual act purely, as pleasure alone. But lovers inevitably became people and emotional involvement followed in one way or another.

Perhaps it should be the Parisian, Jean Eveux. He had aspirations of an imaginative sort. The allure she had for him, powerful enough to pull him across the ocean, was entirely physical. Whether he was a simple pagan or a complex romantic decadent was not clear. As an escort he was highly sophisticated, a connoisseur of foods, wines, entertainments.

She had allowed Jean to proposition her. He had done it with an exquisite recital of clinical detail that might have shocked her if he hadn't been so totally unembarrassed himself. He had analyzed, intellectualized, made a kind of passionate science of sex.

Yet, to embark on a project of exploration of all possible physical joys seemed somehow distasteful. She would become self-conscious; spontaneity would be impossible. It offended some fastidiousness, some inner core of identity. Except for his horror-tinged fascination as a kind of "love machine" he didn't involve any part of her. Simply, she didn't like him as a person.

And there went the possibility of the depersonalized lover. Even in her most wanton moods, she could not totally abandon herself. However much she thought she wanted to reject feeling for the person, she couldn't. Always there was some element in the man that called out her sympathies, her love, or a part of it, even if only temporarily.

Hell! she thought, *what kind of freedom is it if I can't indulge in a natural, physiological, biological function for the sake of releasing tensions, without investing the partner with a meaning in my life?*

Whoever she called would have *no* meaning. Only Vic could command that position. She *would* not betray the truth of that. Still it was a shame. An injustice to people like Kris Drake and Anton Bromley. They believed they had meaning to her. Kris especially thought he could count on her understanding and loyalty, that she believed in him and was rooting for him. As a person, not simply because she had a financial investment in his success. And Anton, as emotionally tough as he was, would be hurt to know that her alliance with his cause was not complete. She had let him take it for granted that she was with him all the way, that even marriage might not be impossible.

Anton had attracted her the first time they had met, at a large backstage party at a musical comedy last fall. Three nights before, Anton had seen his own new show sink without a trace after five performances. Neither critical nor popular acclaim had been his.

The producer of the hit musical had invited Anton to gloat over him. Before he even arrived the half-drunk crowd of nightclubbers and show angels had happily speculated on how sick the occasion would make Anton Bromley. Champagne and venom had flowed in equal parts! Bromley was a has-been; a man without a hit in five seasons; a big head who was going to have to eat humble pie. They couldn't wait to watch his misery—if he had the guts to show up at all. Before he even got there, Nikki began to feel a real affection for him.

Then he walked in, tall and rakish and suave. Her heart had jumped because Anton had the air and the look of her father in his best years. The rival producer sauntered over smugly to rub things in delicately. Anton drank his champagne, smiled and began to congratulate him.

One of those good losers! Nikki had thought, abruptly contemptuous.

She had been about to shrug him off. But as he spoke, with political eloquence, the temper of his remarks changed. She realized his opening had been mere buildup. He proceeded to deliver a detailed criticism of the musical, song by song, skit by skit, production number by production number, plot step by plot step. He traced each element to some other show, which he named specifically in each case. In the end he said the new hit was 80 percent plagiarism, 90 percent cliché, 100 percent dull.

He was 100 percent wrong about the dullness, Nikki felt. Nonetheless, she was struck by his rude honesty and the force of his controlled anger. A man of courage and convictions, she thought exultantly. The other producer, the director, play hacks, songsmiths, stage managers and a host of other men began to shout at him. The angry man-swarm surrounded him and moved with him away from the exit toward the center of the broad, deep stage. The cast, many still in costumes from the finale, began to form a mob around the inner swarm enclosing Anton.

Expecting a physical brawl, Nikki tingled with excitement and wondered if the spike heels of her flimsy, bejeweled evening sandals would hold up. She took off her swoop-brimmed white velvet picture hat and white fur cape and entrusted them to the two men who were more or less her escorts of the evening. Then, glistening in a black silk gown that bared her upper back, shoulders and a deep luscious V between her breasts, she headed for the action, legs flashing in the skirt's high slits, her tautly sheathed hips rolling.

She twisted, elbowed and bumped her way through a mass of leggy dancers in glittering skimpy costumes. She kept brushing their body makeup off her gown and returning the dumb stares of their sensually grease-pained faces with flicking, stormy glances. She got past the men into an open space near the keyboard of a grand piano. Her emotional momentum was too high to note the change in atmosphere.

"A man has a right to speak his mind," she declared loudly, "without being mobbed by bullies!"

There was a hush. Everybody looked at her. Anton raised his brows, then winked, grinning. A man said indulgently, "Other men have the right to answer him, Miss Duquesne. Right, Anton? Where's that table and chair for Mr. Bromley."

Someone sat at the piano. Others came in with a chair and a small table. Functionaries loaded it with tiny sandwiches, canapes, caviar, champagne; Anton was urged to seat himself. The sultry little team of nearly nude belly dancers, Arabina and Arabelle, with sheer black skirts suspended from their hips, jewels in their navels and Cleopatra hair-dos, moved in and simpered at Anton. He stared fixedly past them at Nikki. Slightly breathless, she thought how grand he was, how even handsomer than her father's was his long triangular face, the flaring cheekbones, the high-arching, vaguely Mephistophelean eyebrows.

He visually stroked the aroused loveliness of her face, the long graceful line of her throat, the flesh of her breasts, the curve of her figure. His gaze paused at the diamond and emerald pin at her waist, at the slickly articulated round and V base of her lower stomach, at the pearl wristlet on her long black gloves. He gestured indolently and said quietly, "A chair for the lady, too, please."

She sat with him, sipping wine and nibbling delicacies for almost an hour while a pianist, chorus singers and dancing girls, from Arabina and Arabelle to a frenzied line of bump-grind-twist artists, presented the cream of the show. Interspersing the carnal seduction were earnest words, explanations, rationalizations: if this had been lifted from such and such, such and such had been taken from so and so, which had been stolen from something else before that. . . . And not only was this justified, but *de rigueur*. As Anton Bromley well knew, they said, audiences wanted the familiar, like children demanding the same bedtime story over and over.

Although he smiled and applauded the performers, along with the rest of the crowd, he listened to the talk with growing annoyance.

"You're talking about three-year-olds. Even TV and

Hollywood sometimes aspire a helluva lot higher than that, and they're not clipping the customer seven-seventy. You show off your pretty girls, which is like a lunchroom bragging that it serves bread with its sandwiches. You couldn't do without them, but even they're not displayed for all they're worth. The choreography has no freshness. The costumes are copied. The sets are tired.

"And when we hear songs that are almost but not quite like something heard too many times, it's not refreshing but aggravating, like a singer constantly off-key. Your jokes are predictable, which robs them of their punch lines, so we get none of the release that humor is supposed to provide. We laugh politely, embarrassedly, self-consciously. Skits that are supposed to be light enough to lift us to gaiety are heavy with age, in your show.

"The mood scenes never come close to genuine emotion, let alone moments of magic. The cliché sentiments are only thrown in because they've been successful in other shows. In those shows the sentiments were moving because they were meaningful to a certain character in a specific situation within the created whole of the world of that other play. Those sentiments belong somewhere else, so they are fraudulent within the hodgepodge context you give them.

"Nothing here is original, nothing has been created; the production and direction do not bind the whole together. The libido binds together, according to Freud. It is the impulse and the function of the libido to reach out and touch with love and bind together. Your production is a case in point. It wasn't staged by a man with any love for the theater. . . . Miss Duquesne, I'm leaving and I'd be happy to have you come with me. Will you, please?"

"I will. As soon as I get my things."

They made their way to the stage door. They were going out into the paved areaway between buildings when the other producer hurried out.

"Anton, you didn't mean it. You exaggerated."

"Dramatized is the word we in the theater use," Anton said coldly. He paused under the fire escape and looked at him bleakly. "In the laboratory they'd say 'magnified.'

An enlargement for the purpose of making something clear. I meant it, Mort."

"But not so rough, Anton!"

"You hit. I hit back."

"I apologize. I rubbed it in when you're running in bad luck, like kicking you when you're down."

"Temporarily!"

"Sure! Wait, don't go off. Maybe it is a show I ought to be ashamed of, bu—"

"No maybe."

"But not because I've got no love for the theater. I *had* to have a hit. And not just from hunger. Flops eat you to death. One more, you think," he said emotionally, "and you'll kill yourself. Only you can't."

Anton reached over and gripped his shoulder. "I know. I know."

Embarrassed, Nikki looked away, then moved away, walking slowly out to the sidewalk. She stopped, looked back to see them practically embracing and frowned. When a cab turned into the cross street from Broadway, she hesitated, then hailed it. She'd climbed in when Anton came running and got in beside her.

"Say," he laughed, "you're hard to hold. There's a good cool jazz club downtown. Driver, take us—"

"I" Nikki said abruptly, "gave him the address. Uptown. The very term cool jazz is a contradiction; true jazz being whorehouse hot. The bloodless, passive little people who admire something that's had the passion stripped out of it and sit around listening and feeling cultured and intellectual and 'hip' and 'in' and 'secure' are, to quote a great authority, one hundred percent *dull!*"

"Bravo! What a delivery! A natural born actress! But what did I do? Can I ride with you and try to *undo* it?"

She shrugged, looked out her side window.

"I suppose you reversed your stand on that show one hundred percent."

"Not quite. But I *was* too rough. I understand his problems."

"Spelled d-o-l-l-a-r-s. It gets you here!" She touched the breast of her fur. "The fact is you have the same problem. For a minute when I first came into that scene I thought you were going to put a jeweler's loupe in your eye and appraise the pin I'm wearing. It's real. So's this," she said, touching the pearls on her glove.

She stared at him defiantly, almost bitterly. He frowned and then his face relaxed and he studied her wonderingly for the longest time without a word.

"I don't know," he said finally. "Maybe my resilience is gone. I can't adjust to this mood, this hostility. An hour ago you came charging into my fight to defend me. You looked tame, your eyes shining with admiration. We sat together, the two of us against that whole bunch, and there was a bond, an understanding. We kept looking at each other and liking what we saw and smiling with pleasure of one another. In everything I said, Nikki, you were *with* me. Your face is so damned expressive, so responsive; there couldn't have been any misreading on my part."

"It was nice while it lasted," she allowed. "Now, Anton, we're coming to my street. I have to go right to bed because I'm catching an early plane home to Richmond."

"What? You live there?"

"An hour or so from it. I've got a big farm. It takes all my serious attention. New York's only play." The cab was coming to a stop. "Maybe on my next visit we'll run across each other. Good night."

"I want to know what happened, Nikki. I've got to. You can spare a half-hour. Let me come up. Or are you afraid of me?"

"I can handle any passes. And the jewelry's insured. I simply don't want any more involvement with you just now. Still, if you insist, you may come up."

They sat opposite each other on facing sofas. He lit a cigarette.

"I got into show business while I was a dogface in World War II," he began. "Ever since I was a kid in Sandusky, Ohio, where the word as it existed displeased me greatly, I dreamed of reshaping events, creating new worlds. You see, when I was born—"

"Shall we skip about thirty seven or thirty eight years?"

"You're right. Well, for the past few months I was building up to something; the final few weeks were strenuous, the tension hellish. It all ended a few days ago in sickening failure. I'd been moving around in a black fog, wondering if my luck had run out completely. Tonight, out of nowhere a perfectly beautiful creature came into my life. It was like a sign, a sudden reversal of fortune. I thought it was the *beginning* of something marvelous. And like *that*, it was the *end*.

"Why? First you saw me as a strong man, a fighter. And then I disappointed you greatly, didn't I? By feeling a little pity for Mort, you thought I went soft, became weak, abandoned my principles. Everything you'd hoped I was collapsed. That's it, isn't it. Nikki?"

She bristled. "I didn't know you well enough to build up such hopes."

He looked at her, unconvinced.

"Well," she said nervously, getting to her feet. "Maybe I did have such hopes. Only because—ah, forget it. Please go."

"Because what?" he insisted.

"You look like my father did when he was alive," she said, then did not say aloud, *He, too, was strong and let a fatal softness destroy him.* "You're right that your reconciliation with that man disappointed me. I consider it weak of you. Call me hard, call me pitiless. I don't care. That's how I feel; that's how I judge. And that's my right as a woman."

"By God," he said, grinning and shaking his head. "You could make a job of a role in a certain play I've got under option."

"I'm no actress."

"Listen to me. Buried somewhere in everybody is the capacity for at least one great performance. I've taken people who didn't know they had it in them and I've shaped them and brought out brilliant acting jobs. You've already got a personality that projects. It's magnetic. It's got the so-called star quality. There's an intensity, a fire to you, a dynamic quality that needs only the shaping by an expert hand."

"Forget it."

"I want you to read that play. I'm going to produce it. *You're* going to star in it."

She looked at him suspiciously.

"Have you got the backing?"

He waved a hand. "That, no. Not yet. But wait'll you

read it. You'll realize I won't have trouble raising money."

"It could even be," she said cynically, "that you'd allow *me* to invest in it."

"Oh, wait a minute! Sure, I'd be glad to have your money; but don't be silly. I'm not making a con man pitch and dangling glamour bait about an acting career. I mean it, I want to make an actress out of you. You're a natural, Nikki."

"You can send a copy of the play," she said. "But I have no ambition to be taken over and shaped. Or to say words somebody else puts into my mouth. Or pretend to be another person. I'm Nikki Duquesne, and that's just exactly who I want to be. Thanks just the same."

She went over to the door, opened it and said firmly, "Good night!"

She was in Virginia two weeks. When she returned to the city for a few days, the play script was waiting. She read it at once, called a messenger service and sent it back to Anton's office with a note.

"A.B.: I detest it. N.D."

The messenger brought the script back.

"N.D.: Knew you'd react strongly. Strong play. A.B."

Then, after a lifetime of never seeing him, she ran across him everywhere. He was at the spectacular Garden horse show, a ballet, Russian restaurant, an outspoken off-Broadway shocker, a key club, an Hawaiian restaurant, with one pretty girl after another. She had a feeling of being stalked. She was outwardly cool and polite, but acutely aware of him and fascinated.

They had mutual acquaintances among newspaper and publicity men and Nikki pumped them about him. Some didn't like him personally but the concensus was that he was first-rate professionally; definitely not shifty in financial matters. He was an artist without being arty. His hits, two of which she'd seen and liked, had been distinguished. His only real failure was his last play. In preceding seasons he'd had good shows, modestly successful at the box office without being smash hits.

The one from last year had got off to a slow start, but hung on, picking up steadily, and might have been running yet. Except, through a technicality in his lease, Anton was evicted for the sake of another show which the theater owners judged would make a fortune. (It had lost a fortune, despite big-drum publicity and a month's advance ticket sales.)

The detested script nagged her. She reread it merely to confirm her own judgment. It was strong. Too much so. A sweeping emotional force. She refused to be swept. Her decision was unchanged.

Then, the night before her next return to Virginia something terrifying happened.

She had been in bed sound asleep. She became aware of a slight chill and realized with a shock that the bed covers were off. She was on her back, staring straight up into the darkness, arms extended out from her sides. Her shorty nightgown had worked itself up above her navel. Her knees were raised and open. Obscurely she felt a receding, diminishing wave of sexual sensation, as if someone had been caressing her intimately.

There was an intruder in the bedroom, she thought wildly. Lurking somewhere in the shadows out there beyond the bed, crouched and silent in the dark. She wanted to stretch her arm to the light. A paralysis held her. She mustn't signal she was awake until she had assembled her wits. Her mind was a cataclysm. She couldn't think. Her neck and head became rigid.

Her breathing slowed, almost stopped. She listened and there was no sound, no movement. Even the air, chill on her body, did not stir. She inched her head up, peering. There was an indistinct pattern of massed shadows that she didn't recognize as part of the room and which must be the man. He knew she was awake, looking at him!

Abruptly he touched her privately with something he was holding. Like a phallus made of ice. It seemed to freeze all her body, except the sensitive intimate areas. She thought it was Anton! Anton playing a ghastly joke. Before she knew it she had begun to rush toward an orgasm. She fought it, held it back. If she let it sweep her, it would be so powerful it would shake her body into convulsions that would go on and on. Until she was senseless. Until she was *dead. That's what you are, Anton,* she thought savagely. *Death.*

She kicked him and turned on the light and saw his face. It *was* Anton . . . was *not* Anton. She knew who it was, and he was dead.

She woke and turned on the light and the bedroom was empty. Of course.

And of course Anton was Anton, a person in his own right, his only connection with her father a superficial resemblance. And there was nothing guilty about wanting him to make love to her.

She phoned him. He answered, groggy with sleep.

"Anton," she said huskily, "can you come over?"

"Nikki? . . . What's the matter, Nikki?"

"I want you. Do you want me?"

He came sharply awake.

"Hell, yes! When? *Now?*"

"Now."

She couldn't wait. Her whole system quickened with anticipation. Her desire was stronger than desire. It was a craving, an urgency, a necessity. That morbid dream had risen from some frightening hidden depth within herself which *must be overwhelmed* by a passionate, living heat.

She hurled and kicked the covers away. Lying with her pillowed head turned to a mirror, she raised her body into an arched, coital position, bracing on her shoulders and heels. Watching herself, but imagining he was watching, she stripped off the shorty nightgown's wispy bodice and panty, her feminine hands caressing her breasts and smooth belly and roundly clenched bottom and hips and soft, open thighs. The friction sent thrills over her skin. If only the hands were Vic's. Strong, male hands!

Her eyes flashed with sudden anger. She let her hips drop, bouncing, to the bed and kicked out with both legs, sailing the dainty nightgown to the floor. With a rolling, whipping motion she brought her lithe young body into a sitting position, her long, pretty legs swinging and dropping to the floor. She thrust her slim toes under the fat black pompoms of her red satin mules and stood erect.

She elongated the lines of her stunning, naked body, lifting her exquisite conical breasts so high they trembled. How *dared* Vic Hollister marry anyone else? she thought with reasonless savagery. Her hair, tousled and still warm from the pillow and loose around her cheeks, gave a passionate accent to the stormy beauty of her face. He had betrayed her. Well, two could play that game!

In the bathroom she freshened her face and perfumed herself and began to brush her hair vigorously. Her whole body was too warm. Her mouth was parched. She went to the kitchen, loaded a tall sixteen-ounce glass to the brim with ice cubes and poured in wine, intently watching the purple liquid cascading down over the ice, then she added sparkling water. She took a drink and held it in her mouth enjoying the coldness and sharp flavor for a few seconds before swallowing. She carried the glass to the bedroom and sipped while she prepared for Anton.

She was waiting at her partly open door when Anton stepped off the elevator blowing smoke. He waved, snubbed his cigarette in the sand urn, and came toward her in a long, smooth stride, his topcoat open, hat pushed back.

"Nikki, you're enchanting," he said softly as he came in.

She smiled nervously and shut the door while he put his things on a bench. Her body was completely covered in a lustrous, quilted, blue floor-length robe that rose narrowing from a wide circular hem like a pyramid supporting her throat and head. Her hair was massed out on one side of her head but sleeked tight against the other.

"The imbalanced hair-do," he said, turning and eying her appreciatively, "and the total concealment of everything but your head is damned intriguing."

She gave him a sultry, teasing look. "I thought I'd just be naked when you came, then I thought you might prefer to have a package to unwrap. Do you want a drink?"

"No. I want to kiss you."

He moved quickly, his arms opening and encircling her. Her face lifted, eagerly responsive. He frowned slightly and brought his lips down hard. While he kissed her, his hands stroked up and down her robe, feeling the contours of her body. He withdrew from the kiss, studied her, then kissed her forehead and her cheek. One arm clamped her tighter to him, while he freed the other and stroked her face, very delicately.

"How magnificently you're made. Your bone structure, your texture, your *élan*. I want to look and feel and sense you in every way, Nikki. . . . Maybe I *will* have that drink. This is something I *won't* rush."

"I don't want it rushed either. What kind of drink?"

He told her and while she was fixing it he came and kissed the side of her neck, then the back. His hand slipped in under the front of her robe. She stood very still, staring. As his hand went to her naked breast and fondled and squeezed and stroked, she began to breathe more quickly. He withdrew his hand. She completed the drink.

She stood watching him as he downed part of it, his half-lidded eyes holding unwaveringly to her. He pulled her against him and kissed her mouth, this time thrusting his tongue between her lips and holding the kiss till she was breathless. One of his hands moved inside her robe and stroked downward slowly toward her intimacy.

He broke the kiss and at once kissed her again. Both his hands went in under the robe, glided around her body and stroked and pressed her buttocks. He eased her lower body in against his. Her arms abruptly locked around his waist. She mashed herself against him, feeling his male arousal.

They separated. He finished his drink, walked away, pulling off his tie. He led her over to one of the sofas, and sat her on his lap. He opened her robe and began to kiss her body, and her throat. Time and again he drew her face down and kissed her lengthily.

He put her off his lap, stood up and went to the bedroom and looked in. He motioned his head for her to go in. She nodded and walked over, her mouth feeling swollen and throbbing, her eyes glazed and vaguely stuporous. As she passed him he deftly pulled the robe off her shoulders. She paused. He shook his head.

"Go on. Get on the bed."

She liked his tone of voice and she went and lay as he commanded. She watched him steadily as he undressed. When he was fully naked, she caught her breath sharply.

...ike that?"
...e a good man!"

He stood at the edge of the bed, looking down at her naked body, and she moved herself enticingly, to please him. She smiled and waited. Then he was coming onto the bed. He lay beside her and she stretched herself and turned, rubbing against him with a feline pleasure, her eyes shut, a soft smile on her lips. He stroked her and she caressed him. He kissed her again, then rolled her on her back and lifted her hips and moved in between her thighs. He stared down at her with a certain edge of harshness that made her shiver with delight.

He was moving closer and closer, virile and fiercely hot.

Then he was there! His penetration was controlled, a smooth rhythmic thrust and withdrawal and thrust, deepening in gradual stages. His flanks quivered with tension and there was a brilliance to his eyes and power to his gripping hands and a driving, rising excitement about his lovemaking. He had roused her to fever pitch before he entered and she was far ahead of him. She suddenly caught her breath, gasping with pleasure. She gripped him and held on, her whole being caught in spasms of pure joyous release.

"Happy?" he said hoarsely. For answer she kissed him passionately.

He continued in his strong rhythm, enjoying her and himself and prolonging that joy masterfully. She found herself coming to a peak of pleasure again. . . . Still he was not ready. When he was ready, he increased his tempo to a driving violence that was painful, joyous and irresistible.

When they were lying quietly beside each other in a state of delicious tiredness, she said faintly, "I have been loved. I have really been loved! Oh, Anton, you're wonderful."

"What an experience *you* are, Nikki." He sighed. "Ah-h-h-h, what a woman."

As blissful as it had been, she was not tempted, next morning, to stay over another day. She caught her plane back home right on schedule.

At the airport she let him know she would invest in the play. And she made it clear that his love-making

had had nothing to do with it, that she'd brok[e a cer]-
tain psychological block about it before that.

The next month Anton had $25,000 in checks and
pledges. To raise the balance he planned a series of
professional readings of the play for select groups of
possible backers. At that time she'd been not only clash-
ing with George Penstone and yearning for Vic Hollister, but the problems of her land ensnarled her like
a jungle she was trying to hack through with no com-
pass, no clearing in sight.

She'd fretted about the time wasting uncertainties of
Anton's fund-raising. She wanted the production to get
going without delay. She had meant to put in $5,000.
Then she thought if that much was a good investment,
more would be better. In a flash of combined logic and
madness, she pledged the whole remaining amount he
needed—*$175,000!*

When she informed Vic, he almost went through the
roof of the Hollister Buiding. Certain that she was being
lured by a Svengali confidence man, he went to New
York to see Anton and his lawyer. Actually Anton had
tried to argue Nikki out of going whole hog.

Vic made Anton admit something that Nikki hadn't
considered: Producers' cost estimates were notoriously
unreliable, not deliberate misrepresentations but too
optimistic. Thus there might be additional calls on her
money. The two men had finally teamed up to reason
with her, back her down. Their mistake was treating
her like a child. And Nikki's will, whether or not it was
a will to destruction, had prevailed.

As Vic had warned, unanticipated expenses *had* come
along. As of this minute she was in for—with no guar-
antee that more wouldn't be required—a total of *$212,-
458.70!* A sobering sum.

The out-of-town tryouts had been postponed three
times. Maybe the show would be ready to open in
Philadelphia next week. Maybe not. Anton and Kris
were doing their best. An ironic thought made her grin
tightly. Her enemy, Penstone, who only yesterday had
tried to rape her, would like to break her. But he hadn't
been able to get her land. Anton and Kris were friends
—lovers—who cared for her and labored in her cause
as well as their own. But if the show didn't open, she'd

take a dead loss. That would wipe out her financial reserves and do what her enemy had failed to do—cause her to lose her beloved land and home.

Not that she would blame anybody but herself. Early in the venture she had resolved that no matter how anxious she might become about things she would never reproach or accuse Anton. She would be too big for that! And what had Nikki "Too Big for That" Duquesne done, not once but several times? Why, of course she had lashed out with reproaches and accusations.

And what had Anton done—damn him, bless him? He'd absorbed it, his confidence unruffled. He'd been strong, stronger than she. He had not lashed back in any way, but had soothed and comforted and *understood* her. He knew and valued women. Specifically *her*, Nikki felt. He had the perception to see through to her inner moods. As a lover he was an artist and could transform her from indifference to sweetness to submission to passion. His was the initiative, the carrying force. He remained comfortingly above her in command, however swept he was by his own desire.

Anton was the lover she wanted tonight, she decided. One who would dominate. She went to the phone and changed her mind. What the *real* Nikki required was a lover to give her the thrilling feel of naked power as well as ecstasy. She would call Kris Drake.

Instead, she went to the little bar she'd installed in a corner. She poured a double shot of straight whisky, drank it raw. Then, grinning, she walked calmly over to the phone.

She would summon them *both*!

Chapter Seven

Anton got there first. He came down the hall in a hurry. Nikki, in silver lounging pajamas, her hair loose and sultry around her cheeks, watched him with a faint smile. He frowned at her and stepped past her into the apartment.

"A man full of agitations and displeasures," Nikki said with soft, affectionate mockery.

"Kris phoned me that you invited him, too," he said, looking at her sternly. "Is he here?"

"Not yet." She grinned at him.

Anton reached past her, slammed the door shut and locked it. He turned away to put his hat and coat down, saying briskly, "Good. He's got to memorize new lines of a scene we just rewrote this afternoon, and he's due for an early rehearsal—and believe me that boy can use all the rehearsal he can get." He turned back to her, smiled broadly. "Darling, you look delicious. It's wonderful to see you. Good flight, I hope."

"M'm-h'm. You're looking nice and edgy and vital," she said, moving easily in against him as he stepped forward and kissed her softly. "The play shaping up? Is he—how do you say—'taking the stage?'"

"He did *once*. Which shows he *can*. Two afternoons ago we ran through all three acts in sequence. Without sets, props, costumes; but all the lines, positions, entrances, exits and general business were there. It was a complete performance, a fused continuing whole. We didn't stop for flubs or to polish an individual bit or scene. When we've done this before, Kris was—well, Kris. Passive, flowing along with the thing, trying to keep up. But this time he really took the stage. It perked up the whole cast. Gave them confidence, almost for the first time."

"Marvelous," she said excitedly. "How did he do in that tricky second act scene where the real character begins to show through?"

"It still confuses him. He glimpses it, then gets self-conscious. He starts to do the one thing he was never meant to attempt: *think*." He grinned malevolently.

"About his image?" She giggled. "His Hollywood image?"

"Exactly. In those beautiful dummy roles of his, evil was no part of him; that was for ugly people. He could show bad-*boy* but never bad-*man* traits. He's scared of the sonofabitchery in this character. He worries that the retarded adolescents who idolize him may find out about it."

"Could a success in this role ruin the image?"

"Hell, no. Not one in a hundred thousand of his morons will see the play. The rest will know he's had a Broadway success. And Broadway has prestige, the more so the farther you get from it. When he comes, Nikki, you can say hello and send him back to his hotel."

"I can but I don't intend to," she said.

Smiling to herself, she started toward the bar, moving with a teasing, feline grace, her hips rolling.

When Anton caught her and spun her around, she laughed gleefully. He clamped her body to his and kissed her mouth, bearing down hard. He tried to deep-kiss her. She turned her face and freed herself.

"Don't be overpossessive," she said lightly. She went on to the bar.

"You're not to walk in that inciting alley-cat way around him."

"You incited?" She grinned. "Jealous? Want brandy?"

"Nikki, what're you up to, inviting both of us?"

Busy pouring brandy, she shrugged, then pushed the snifter toward him. She smiled up at his bleak face.

"I couldn't decide between you," she said innocently. She pouted. "You're looking mean. Kris will look charming."

He swirled the brandy around and around, watching her.

"Nikki. I've fought to get Kris in confident balance and keep him there. This could topple him. It's no time to put the poor devil into a sexual competition that will shake hell out of his ego."

"We'd better see to it that he wins, h'm?"

He laughed. "By God, Nikki, you're half-drunk!"

"Oh, that big laugh. As if you own me. He thinks I belong to him. The joke is, I'm nobody's. Or anybody's I choose to be at any time."

"Nikki, cut it out. I *love* you."

"Love. That's a good last-resort word to trot in when you're *determined* to have your way."

"I mean that word. I love you, Nikki."

"And because of the subjective condition you're in—or claim to be in—I'm supposed to feel a great obligation and surrender my freedom. Including freedom of choice," she said coolly, but he was gazing at her with such earnest intentness that she softened. "Oh, please, Anton, don't look at me that way. Don't be unhappy." The buzzer sounded. "That'll be Kris. I invited him and I'm not going to turn him away. That's how it is."

Whenever Kris Drake was going to be on public display, he climbed into built-up shoes, cunningly tailored wedge line suit, put on eye makeup, dental caps and a "rug" to hide the slight retreat of his hairline. But Kris didn't need the props. Though not so tall, his physique was well proportioned with fine masculine lines that showed, Nikki admitted, to even better advantage when he was naked. His face, including the natural line of his thick dark brown hair, was strikingly made, the forehead smooth, eyes widely set, the nose elegantly carved, the chin-jaw structure strong. His mouth was wide, the smile with his own good teeth or dental caps was disarming. He had a certain easy animal grace and charm when animated. But without makeup his eyes were dull.

She had actually met Kris before she knew Anton. It had been at a lavish banquet and ball in a midtown hotel. She had been—with the aid of Tiffany, Balenciaga and a Fifth Avenue salon—at her best, surrounded by a coterie of admirers.

Kris Drake, the center of another, much larger circle, had kept eying her, trying to get a response. When he finally realized she wasn't being coy, his vanity was pricked. He plowed his way through to her and announced, "Redheads are my weakness. I go for all redheads."

"Oh," she cried in mock despair. "I was *that* close to Paradise. Mr. Kris Drake, dream man of every girl alive, chose little *me*! Because of the color of my hair. And I am not *worthy*. It's a wig!"

While she talked she saw from his expression that he hadn't expected such response. He had made himself available and here she was treating the gift lightly, even scornfully. When she finished, he laughed hollowly, looking confused. Then, as if she had blown up in her lines, he fed her the cue again, repeating his opening words exactly, "Redheads are my weakness. I go for all redheads."

Nikki, in turn, repeated her speech as exactly as she

remembered it. The men she'd been dancing, flirting and drinking with moderately had been watching Kris with curiosity, then amusement, finally with a certain easy contempt.

He looked back across his shoulder as if looking for a rescue party of writers and directors to give him the words, mood, movements necessary to bring off this scene. He had arrived at the ball with his manager, a woman from his agency, his press agent, two clever men from his studio's promotion department, executive and wives of a theater chain and film distributor, starlets, models, clusters of society girls and women. He had been securely insulated but he had gone truant and here he was confronted by downright irreverence.

He laughed. "A wig!" He waited for appreciation of his cleverness in vain. Then he topped himself. "I'm from Missouri." He reached out toward her head.

"Don't touch!" she said so sharply that he blinked and pulled back. "This," Nikki said casually to the man beside her, "is our dance." She moved away.

An hour later he cut in on her, dancing.

"I found out your name. It's Nikki Duquesne."

"I already knew that. The music has stopped. Please take me to my table."

"Why, the music didn't stop!"

"With you I don't hear it. Is that too subtle? If you want to be left standing out here alone that's up to you."

"Wait . . . I'll take you back if that's how you want it. Listen, I didn't mean I only went for you because you've got red hair. I apologize. O. K.? Are you free tomorrow night?"

"I'm flying to Paris. And when I come back I won't be free either."

"Why don't you like me?"

"You *really* want to know?"

She gave him a flicking glance and grinned. He frowned uncertainly.

"All right." Nikki laughed. "I promise not to tell you if you promise to leave me alone."

He didn't leave her alone. He found out her address. He phoned and telegraphed. He inundated her apartment with flowers, which she immediately forwarded to hospitals. She had to credit him with persistence at least, and dated him four or five times. He tried to be amusing but he was dull; his romantic overtures didn't touch her. Only because she felt a little sorry for him did she allow him even a good-night kiss.

He managed to be where she was regularly and as regularly she gave him cutting pieces of her opinion of him. Meantime she'd met Anton and put her money into his play. Anton was trying to cast it and was not only busy night and day in consultations, negotiations with the Guild, agents and actors, but he made frequent trips out of town.

He was in Chicago signing the second-lead actress the midnight Kris came into Sardi's. The restaurant, a mecca for show people and glamour-struck tourists, featured photos and caricatures of theatrical luminaries, including Anton's, along its walls. Kris had been, she heard, angling to get his picture hung. He came regularly and was a big enough name to attract considerable attention.

Nikki was listening fascinatedly to the old-time press agent Anton had retained to publicize the play. Kris seated himself in their booth, uninvited. After a little banter the press agent left. Nikki looked at Kris exasperatedly.

"You're spreading a blight of dullness over my life," she began and proceeded to give him a tongue-lashing that almost drew blood.

"By God, you're a rough little devil!" He gazed at her admiringly. "Also an angel, I hear. That's what I wanted to talk about. You're backing Anton Bromley's new play. Well, the male lead's not cast. And *I'm* available."

"Oh, no!" She shut her eyes. She opened them and stared. "Have I neglected to mention that I endured two of your movies and consider you an actor of unparalleled incompetence?"

He grinned. "You didn't neglect it. Only, Nikki, it wasn't *me*. The roles were bad. I want to show what I can really do. Broadway's the place."

"I take it that Hollywood's not so passionate about you at the moment."

"That's no joke," he said gloomily. "Listen, Nikki . . .

please sit down . . . don't go . . . The problem between you and me, I realize now, is a lack of communication."

She got up and started out.

"I must go. Good night."

He followed her outside. She wouldn't let him in her cab. He got another and followed. He made such a silly spectacle in front of Jack Tenn, pleading to come up and "communicate," that she was embarrassed for him and let him come up.

By "communicate" he meant, of course, to talk about himself. He'd been born in Hollywood. His father had been a stunt man, his mother a retired circus aerialist. Both had been, Nikki gathered, highly energetic, emotionally uninhibited and practically fearless. An older sister and younger brother had, he claimed, inherited all the parents' virtues and got 99 percent of the parental love and approval. He himself had been neglected, unloved, barely tolerated by his beautiful, high-tempered mother and tough, impatient father.

Kris stated this as fact. He seemed totally unaware that his every childhood recollection gave evidence to the contrary. In fact, the picture that emerged was of the *favorite* child, who felt abused when he got anything less than 100 percent of everybody's attention.

He'd been unusually attractive and had appeared in scores of pictures before he was twelve. The adult world smiled upon him; his immediate contemporaries loathed him. His teens, without a career, had been dismal. In his early twenties he again got a long-term contract with a big studio. He played bits and marked time and was, unknown to him, held like a sword over the head of a currently popular but strong-headed star. That star got troublesome once too often and the studio rushed Kris into his shoes in a leading role. The picture made money and the fan mail gushed in. The studio began the big buildup to make him a solid star.

"That's how they used to do it in the good old days," he said unhappily. "The star system was *the* way. Everybody knew that. But politicians and radicals down in Washington tried to kill the industry. They wouldn't let studios own theaters any more, so they couldn't afford to make as many pictures, because who'd buy them unless they had to? You know.

"So people lost faith in the star system. You couldn't be secure. The studio wasn't too sure if they ought to keep building me up. Now it's still all up in the air. All this artiness, and these independent producers, and foreign pictures. Now, is that Americanism? I ask you. It gets so your own studio is looking at their own stars like they've got no class.

"Why, I was always loyal, always did a good job. Never delayed production schedules or had temperament or cost them a lot of money. I went any place they sent me to plug the picture, always cooperative. What does it count for? I tell you you can't count on anybody.

"Why, the head of the studio himself who has said to me a hundred times, 'Kris, you're like my own son,' and who I've been loyal to and given all that was asked said to me," Kris said agitatedly, " 'You read the Bible story about the prodigal son, boy?' I said, 'Yes, but what?' and he said, 'He went off. *Did* something. He came back with something added. That's why he was the most beloved. Why don't you go make an arty Eyetalian picture? Or marry Brigitte Bardot or something? Or, who knows, maybe your name in lights will get dim. Everybody's gotta hustle these days, boy.' "

"Look, Kris," Nikki said seriously. "I can't get you into this play. Casting is in Mr. Bromley's hands entirely."

"All you would have to do is get him to let me read. I can *do* something. I'm not just profile. It's not my fault I look too pretty to take serious. I can *act*. Nikki, you understand what it's like to be good-looking. I know you understand me. And you're not after anything. I can trust you. If you say you know I can do it, it'll be so. You're concerned about me. You wouldn't light into me the way you do if you didn't feel for me."

She looked away uncomfortably. She'd been sitting curled in a chair, with Kris on one of the sofas. She sat up, put on her shoes.

"I've got some sweet rolls I'll warm up and make us some coffee."

He came out and sat at the dinette, smoking and watching her.

"This feels wonderful. Just sitting here, watching you. You're such a wonderful girl. Right from the first when you gave me that little roughing up because I got too big for my britches and said the wrong thing about your hair, I knew you were the one girl for me. When I'm around you I don't feel wolfish. I wouldn't make a move you didn't permit.

"If you would just turn around from that oven, Nikki, and look at me in that gorgeous, scornful, mean way, and then smile at me! Nikki, will you?"

There was a poignancy, a sort of defenselessness about him. She felt a curious pang of tenderness in her breast. She bit her lip. Then she straightened and turned and frowned at him. He gazed solemnly with wide eyes, looking up at her. Then slowly, she smiled, sensing its obscure meaning of forgiveness to him.

The softening of his face was so beautiful, so tender that she went to him at once. She bent, pursing her lips and he lifted his mouth. She kissed him and stroked his face with both hands. His arms went around her and she straightened slightly, and drew his head to her breast and held it. She felt choked. He was so vulnerable, so childlike, so weak, so *inadequate* . . . and for that very reason she loved him in that moment.

She had to break away and hurry to the stove. He got up and followed her. He put his arms around her waist and leaned forward and nuzzled his cheek to hers. She smiled softly.

"Go sit down," she said after a moment.

As they ate the rolls and drank the coffee she wanted to break the mood, but it was hard.

"Kris, don't feel so strongly and foolishly about me. I would like to help you, but honestly, all I can do is speak to Anton. It'll be up to him entirely."

"Nikki, I'm still a draw. He'll understand that. I'm B.O. I'd be a pull, a real asset to your play. And I swear to God I *know* I can act. I want you to understand that. I *know*. . . ."

He did something astonishing when they returned to the front room. He took off his shoes. "Look at those built-up heels . . . I'm not really tall." Then he plucked at the edge of his toupé and ripped it off, setting his hairline back half an inch. "See?" He turned his head and ducked it. When he turned back, the dental caps were off. He smiled, tapped his teeth. "These are the real ones, some of them are crooked. I want you to *know* about me, Nikki."

"Why the hell did you do that!" she cried. "Why do you want to debase yourself?"

He came to her chair and knelt before her, and stared into her eyes. "You're beautiful. I want you so much!"

He eased forward and she moved to him. He seized her and kissed her fervently. He pawed at her dress front, and Nikki hastily opened it. He kissed and fondled her breasts. The power of his need for her love was irresistible.

"All right," she whispered. "All right, you poor darling . . . Come on."

She moved swiftly to the bedroom and he followed. She undressed herself rapidly. He undressed more slowly, staring fixedly at her. When they were both naked, she moved to him, and merged her body with his and he stroked her and kissed her. She drew them toward the bed, whispering love words and petting him. Then she became aware of a slackening of his passion.

"What's wrong, Kris?" she whispered anxiously.

"I'm all right." His body belied it. "It's—I don't know. All this seriousness between us . . . something's changed."

"And now you don't want me?"

"More than anything. But . . . I don't know . . ."

She urged him onto the bed. They lay together and she caressed him, murmuring softly, lovingly. But he was tepid. All his urgency was gone.

"I know," she hissed. She rolled away, jumped up. He got up, too, and watched her nervously.

"What're you doing?"

She was probing through the clothes closet. She located a leather suit belt, yanked it off. It was red, two inches wide. She dangled it. She moved toward him in a semi-crouch.

"I quit abusing you," she snapped. "I started loving you, submitting to you. You need the feel of *pain*! Mastery."

He took a half-step back. His eyes brightened. He shook his head no, but a grin tickled the corner of his mouth. She kept coming.

Suddenly she raised the belt. She brought it down slashingly so that it curled around him. She struck him seven or eight cracking blows, then flung the belt to the floor. They stared at each other. Welt lines showed on his body. And more, he was roused to sexual intensity!

Silent, Nikki pointed to the bed. He climbed onto the bed. She joined him. He made love to her passionately.

Afterward, he sighed blissfully.

"Oh, Nikki! You know how to make me happy. Oh, you *know*."

She rolled, got on her hands and knees beside him and glared down at him. "Listen to me! You're not going to get that ever again. Understand? You'll be man enough to be your own whip! Hear?" The simple lashing of her words and her dominance was enough to rouse him. He tried to make love to her again, immediately. She wouldn't let him.

He never forgot that beating. He tried repeatedly to goad her into another one. But he had to be satisfied with less, from his viewpoint, on the infrequent occasions when he got anything at all.

Anton had let him read. He decided that Kris *did* have the potential to bring off the role and/or to bring in paying customers. . . .

Nikki heard the elevator coming up and started over to open the hall door for Kris. Anton stopped her.

"Nikki, this is no good!" he said in a low, urgent voice. He stared intently into her eyes. "Your taste for people you can dominate, for the likes of Kris Drake, is displaced, overblown maternalism."

"Confine your displaced, overblown *pat*ernalism to your work, which is *not* psychoanalysis," she said slashingly and yanked open the hall door.

Kris had come off the elevator and was moving toward her, carrying a picnic hamper and an armload of red roses. Nikki beamed at him.

"Kris! You darling, look what you've brought me!"

"Hi, doll. I brought a treat for my treat," he said. But, seeing Anton watching hawkishly, his smile was wary. She went on tiptoe and gave him a quick kiss. She took the flowers, exclaiming over them, and went for a vase while he took the hamper to the dinette, explaining, "Chicken and the works. For two . . . Hello, Anton."

"Hi," Anton said. "You get the grub at that Times Square shooting gallery with the caramel corn and rotisserie out front?"

"Don't be funny," Nikki called from the kitchen where she was putting the flowers in a vase. She brought the vase in and placed it on a table.

Kris, in slacks, comfortable loafers, cable-stitch green sweater, stood taking off his belted trench coat and fedora.

"Some men bring a woman gifts. Others bring her unpaid bills," Kris said, and made a sort of exit to the closet where he hung his coat neatly.

"Good line. Tell Joe Embersall I said so," Anton said drily, referring to the play's author.

"You think I can't make up my own lines?"

"I know it, Kris. And you know I know it."

"Let Kris alone," Nikki said. "Let's eat."

"Just us," Kris said firmly, and strode out to the kitchen. "I have to talk to you alone."

"Nikki," Kris said, *sotto voce*, "Please send him away! He doesn't love you or need you the way I do. Dearest. . ."

He started to take her in his arms to kiss her. Anton appeared. He looked at them icily.

"Go sit down," Nikki told Kris and smiled at Anton.

At the table Kris ate hungrily, Nikki nibbled politely. Anton drank and badgered Kris. When she got up and went in to the bar and poured herself another drink, they both followed her. Kris managed to slip his hand around and pat her bottom without Anton seeing. Going back to the table, she swished, aware that both were watching, lusting for her.

"Your whole trouble is trying to become an actor," Anton said.

"Trying to become!" Kris cried indignantly.

"Yes. Trying—belatedly—to become an actor."

Nikki laughed. "Kris, he told me how marvelously you took the stage two days ago. So don't let him bother you."

"I'm talking to a member of my cast, Nikki!" Anton said coldly.

"Don't use that tone with me!" she said. This made Kris smirk, so she tilted the advantage back to Anton.

"He's got every right to talk to you as your director. If you're on top of that role, it's because he has shaped you. Given you an understanding of it. Stripped away most of those cute Hollywood mannerisms you were trying to drag into the characterization."

The discussion resumed in the front room, with Kris and Anton on facing sofas. Nikki, sitting with her feet tucked up in a big chair, was with neither of them. She was, instead, the audience and judge they both appealed to, the focus of conflict and desire. The role thrilled her.

She allowed Kris to fetch her a drink. She awarded Anton a private smile, a kind of assurance, but not quite. At another time she gave Kris an especially seductive little business with the eyes. It was fun; she felt woozy; she had yet another drink.

"Your main trouble," Anton told Kris, "is that your experience has been that of a personality, a performer. The difference between performer and actor is roughly this: The actor is aware of himself as the person he's portraying. He lives in the world of the play and responds to the people and events within that world. The performer is audience-orientated, aware primarily of the onlookers. Take a man and wife in love and in a fight that can end in a divorce that would be tragic for both. They are in their house, in front of the picture window. Neighbors are watching but the *actor* will scarcely be aware of it. The *performer* will maneuver around so that his best profile is to the window."

"But there *is* an audience. Maybe not for Bromley productions, but—"

"As another example of the performer, the profile, the personality, the mugger, in action. He is listening to pointers which may affect his whole future career. He has the opportunity to make an obvious cute remark. He makes it, he glances over to see if Nikki realizes what an enchanting lad he is; he turns on the boyish lopsided grin. Gone is the illusion of a serious artist anxious to understand and master his craft."

"Well, now, just wait one minute, Anton; we're here on a social, personal occasion."

"It's getting late. I'll bet you've not memorized those new lines."

"I'll bet I have."

"Yeah, let's hear 'em?"

Kris reeled them off.

"My parrot could do better. Are we going to have to waste the company's time tomorrow again while we're forcing you to put meaning to your sounds?" Anton got angrily to his feet, went to the bar and got himself a drink. "Playtime's over. Play time is here. We've got less than a week. I won't delay that Philadelphia tryout again. In fact, Mister, I can't. The deal with the theater there is set. You buckle down. I can't order, but I can strongly advise you to get home and go to sleep with that script and be ready tomorrow morning."

"I'll be fine. You seem edgy yourself. Why don't you get home and get in *your* sack time."

Nikki began to giggle. They both looked at her.

The wrangle shifted to problems of the play itself and moved to the collisions between and temperamental problems of other members of the cast, then to troubles with rewriting and bits of staging business. Then, with Nikki getting into it, the talk was of sets, costume fittings, transportation, advertising, publicity.

Underlying it all was the personal, sexual rivalry. She became sleepy. Each of the men alerted, knowing one might be chosen. Neither would volunteer to leave. She got up and started to her bedroom. They both tried to follow. It was becoming farcical. Finally she became aggravated with the whole situation and knew it had been a mistake.

"Either both of you go home or both of you stay or flip a coin. I'm tired. Good night," she said testily.

She went in the bedroom, locked the door and went to bed. She lay listening for a while, sure that neither of them would let the other stay alone and that they would both go. She was really very tired and dropped off to sleep.

It was almost four o'clock when she woke. Frowning and wondering, she crossed and unlocked the door and peered out. A lamp was on. They were both still there. Sprawled out and sound asleep. The sudden ridiculousness of it made her want to laugh.

One of Anton's eyes opened. He was up like a panther. He came swiftly and silently to the door. He pushed her back into the bedroom, shut the door. He picked her up bodily, carried her to the bed.

He put her on her back and stripped down her silk pajama pants, stroking and kissing her thighs as he bared them. He pulled up the coat and kissed her belly and then grinned gloatingly at her and lay on top of her and kissed her mouth and petted her face.

"You're mine, dearest doll. *Mine!*"

Without undressing, he shifted himself and opened her thighs and entered her swiftly. She arched herself, accommodating her body to his intense, thrilling heat and urgency. They were both aware of Kris out there, liable at any moment to wake.

"Fast, this time," he whispered, and it was as if they were involved in a delicious conspiracy.

"Yes!" she answered excitedly. The fury of his tempo, she thought ecstatically, was even more stimulating than his usual control. There was a particular keenness and feel of suspense in knowing they might get caught. She felt herself racing wildly. She was ready to burst.

Then it was over in one glorious burst of sensation. She lay panting, throbbing, completely satisfied. Anton was on his feet. She reached out and gripped his hand. He bent and kissed her. Then he buried his face in the pillow and laughed.

"You villain," she whispered, then had to smother sudden giggles.

There was a sound from the other room. Anton tensed, straightened. He hurried to the door. He went out. Nikki crept to the door and listened.

"Ah . . . Kris! Finally you're awake. Lord, what I've been through. She was sick as a dog. The plane trip and those drinks. She called out in terrible pain. Man, how could you have failed to wake when that little girl needed someone? I *finally* got her calm. Luckily I had some of my yellow pills. I think they'll put her to sleep." There was a light rap on the door. "Nikki? Asleep yet?"

She didn't answer. "I guess the pills have done the trick. C'mon, Kris, let's get out of here. C'mon."

"I guess we'd better."

When they were gone she had a sudden distasteful

image of Anton's slickness. And Kris's gullibility was outrageous. She felt disgusted with them both. Or rather, with all three of them, including Nikki.

Chapter Eight

The knowledge that she *must* get *home* came to Nikki abruptly. Immediately she began to act upon it. And two days sooner than she'd planned she boarded an early morning flight and left New York.

But New York didn't leave her. It—or rather that microscopic-turned-gigantic cell of it, *A Garden of Weeds* by Joseph Embersall, an Anton Bromley Production starring (?) Kris Drake—had, by some insidious osmotic process, surrounded and enclosed her. She was tense throughout the flight.

She left the plane at Richmond airport, looking strained, feeling edgy. She wouldn't—couldn't relax, she knew, till she was *there*—home, safe on her own land. There was a heaviness, obscure and dark, in her chest. She drew her breath deeply but couldn't get enough. She hurried through the terminal, her eyes flicking nervously, seeing little.

She must get her car. Make the hour-plus trip. She'd cut the time to under an hour, she thought. She blinked, shook her head. No, that was reckless thinking, *wreck* thinking. She was suddenly dreadfully afraid. She must be calm, must steady herself. Or she might *never* see home again.

There was a burning in the corners of her eyes. Her vision filmed over. She stopped beside a window and just stared out at acres of parked cars. Their glass and paint and chrome caught the warm sunlight in hundreds of stabbing fragments, harsh and impersonal. Her fingers were cold. Her hands were shaky. She walked on very slowly.

She drove very carefully. It was two hours before she came onto the country road beside her land. It was rolling and lovely and warm and bright with the color of life. Here and there a worker on a tractor or wagon or piece of field equipment saw her, waved and shouted and she answered. Her foreman in a jeep with three field hands emerged and hailed her and vanished again around a curve of roadway. Her purebred dairy herd was grazing a sloping pasture.

Nearing the white horse barns, she saw her beautiful thoroughbred horses, mares and foals. Two mares stood with their muzzles in the clean water of a big trough. Another was rolling herself happily in the big sand pit. Nikki smiled, thinking, *I know just how you feel*. . . .

She turned at the main gate and drove up and around the white-washed gravel drive to the main house.

She stopped her car and got out and stood looking toward the whiteness of the apple orchard, breathing its sweetness.

She entered the house and sang out to the cook and the general maid and embraced them both. She went up to her rooms and opened the windows and stood gazing and filling herself with the sight and joy of everything.

Here was her identity, her balance, her goodness and constructive power. *There,* in that well-named *Garden of Weeds* world of illusion and artifice she was out-of-balance, neurotic.

Destructive. She had left the situation worse than she'd found it, imposed added stress on it. If that production held together, it would be in spite of her. She would *deserve* to lose . . . *everything!*

Everything? Her jaw slackened and dropped open. She stared, an expression of mindless wonder not unlike idiocy on her face. *I could,* she thought, *I really could lose everything*. She had known it, of course. But not in her vitals. She blinked. She shook her head. She paced away nervously, beginning to undress and change clothes.

Nobody would be sorry for her. They would gather round saying, *told you so* . . . *warned you* . . . *serves you right*. They would, she thought in a mood of sweet martyrdom, hurl cruelties after her as she walked away, small and alone; and when, exhausted and heart-broken she fell, there would be none among them to come to her. Unless she was dressed like this, she thought, shattering the mood with a mirrored glimpse of herself stripped to black lace panties and bra.

Where had that mawkish, self-pitying little fantasy come from, she wondered fretfully? Ah, yes! From pre-kindergarten days when her mother used to read or tell her all those bedtime stories. They'd usually been fun stories. But now and then there'd been a sad-sweet tale with the deep and gentle power to make her cry.

She wanted to cry now, she knew. Lie on that bed and cry herself to sleep. So that when she woke all her worries would be gone! By magic? . . . good fairies? . . . pink bunnies? . . . Santa Claus? she thought derisively.

Oh, what hell she'd given her beleaguered father for rearing her in a tradition dappled with fairy tales and pretty falsifications of harsh reality. He had called it protecting and cherishing; she, in the mood of a snapping crocodile, had labeled it stifling and crippling. Well, damn it, it had been. She wasn't ready to write *The Case of the Crocodile Who Bit Off More Than She Could Chew*.

If she was going to indulge in tears, she thought, getting into denim pants, shirt and suede jacket, she'd better get it done fast. Because there'd be a multitude of details to go into with her foreman. Inevitably a few minor but not unimportant decisions would have to be made. There was correspondence to attend to, record entries to be made, bookkeeping to be brought up to date, checks to deposit and to make out.

From Vic's office there might be some official government reports or forms made out and awaiting her signature. If so, there'd be a brief note in Vic's hand. The prospect made her smile. She hurried out and down the stairs to her office in the library. There was nothing from Vic.

She was occupied with routine matters till late afternoon. Then, after dinner, while it was still light she went down to the horse barns with Jockey Club registration forms to get precise descriptions of two of her recent foal crop. She was finishing the second one and trying to draw and describe the forehead marking, uncertain whether it was a blaze or star, when Penstone drove up.

"Oh!" she said exasperatedly. She got up from the bale of hay where she'd been sitting crosslegged and got a pitchfork.

"You want me to tend to him, Miss Duquesne?" the groom who was holding the foal asked, grinning.

"No. Don't you worry, Jim. Penstone, what do you want?" she said, walking to his car with the fork. He stayed in the seat.

"I want permission to make a social call up at the house this evening."

"You've got your damned nerve!"

"I know. I know. What I want to come for is to offer a humble apology."

"I let you be humble and kiss my foot, but you got incensed and out of hand. Go home."

"I promise I never will get rough no more. Leave me come. Please . . . Say, ain't he a little beauty, that blaze-faced foal? I watched him several times and I can tell you something about him. You had him set on his feet, didn't you? When he was born? Right? He couldn't get up and you helped him?"

"How did you know that? How could you tell?"

"I got an eye. Will you leave me come? About an hour? Leave me get right with you, Nikki, please."

She hesitated. "Oh, all right."

When he left, she questioned the barn foreman and the groom. So far as they knew no one had told Penstone about that particular colt's inability to get to its own feet. It was her policy to make them get up by themselves, and find the mare's teat unaided, too. But this one had tried and flopped and tried and flopped for over an hour. Its distress had made her weaken. She'd had the men set the little newborn creature on its feet and later guide it to nourishment.

It rather impressed her that Penstone had detected the facts about the animal. She walked slowly back to the house thinking about him. Whatever else might be said about him, he was real, a part and parcel of the reality of the earth itself. He was primitive, crude, ugly, yes; but solidly anchored in fact, not fantasy. He lived an authentic life, not given over to the wispy, shifty artificialities of show business.

She didn't bother to dress. She waited on the veranda,

sitting relaxedly and feeling the quiet peacefulness of the countryside. Kris, even Anton, would be totally lost here. They wouldn't know the difference between growing oats and wheat, probably wouldn't even recognize the threshed grain or know straw from hay or nutrient grasses from weeds. . . . *A Garden of Weeds.*

And worst would be the pride they would feel about their ignorance. Once or twice they'd revealed their fundamental stupidity by making stale rustic-type jokes about farms. As if cities could exist without farms, as if the docile, dreary, semiliterate, narrow, parochial drones who inhabited cities were superior in anything but numbers. And the Broadway world was in some ways the most restricted and airless of the lot, the *least* alive. Actors particularly were imitations of people, and generally distorted, neurotic people at that.

Penstone drove up to the end of the veranda and got out, wearing a well-made dark blue suit, a neat, striped tie, a well-styled hat. He had on new shoes and he carried a large box of candy. He smiled and put the candy on the table by her elbow.

"Can I sit down?"

"Yes." She indicated the chair across the table. They both sat facing out from the veranda, not looking at one another.

"As I said, Nikki, I want to make a full apology. I am very sorry I broke in on you. And I never had no right to try to force myself on you in that personal way."

"You mean trying to rape me? But let it go. All right, Penstone, I accept the apology."

"I've got a real serious feeling about you. I never met a woman I cared more about. That don't make no difference to you, I know it don't. So what I come about I want to say careful.

"You and me, combined as a team, would have the greatest land holdings in these parts. Quite a bit of what you done on your place is worth adopting to my land. Operations, when they're consolidated, can be cheaper. And it takes a man to boss men. A woman that didn't have all the problems of keeping a place running would have a lot of freedom. And she could go most any time she'd like to most any place she'd want to.

"And I got no use for the double standard. If a woman has got her heart set on variety and playing around, and if she goes off to get it, that's her business.

Nikki gradually sat forward in her chair, and turned her head toward him and just sat staring.

"Penstone, are you proposing to me?"

"Yes."

He looked at her. His face was solemn, his fat cheeks a little slack.

"You didn't say no yet, Nikki."

"I'm too flabbergasted."

She leaned back in her chair and stared at nothing, a faint grin on her lips. After a while she said, "You're the damnedest single-mindedest cuss I ever heard of, Penstone. You've got a fixation about this land of mine."

"It ain't just that!" he protested. "It ain't really that at all. I love you."

"You know, George, I halfway believe you do. Or a quarter-way."

"You can believe it whole-hog way. You're one helluva woman. Now I know you never could *love* a fella like me. But you could *put up* with me. And I'd give you some happiness. You'd be surprised how much I could give you, the way a woman likes it. And I mean it about if you'd want to fool around, you could. Just so you never done it with nobody around these parts and made a fool out of me.

"I wouldn't get rough with you. I know you'd be fair and square and give me something on the bargain. And I could take all the bother off your shoulders. And you could live just as free, practically, as you do now. Now don't just say no, don't say *nothing* right this minute. Wait and think about it a few days. Just leave it lay, don't throw it out yet. Don't say no till you've thought about it."

Near the end he talked fast, leaving no gap for an answer, and loud, as if drowning out the *No, No, No* she must be saying.

But wasn't saying. The presumption of this animal, still practically on all fours, daring to propose to her was just too incredible. She was neither indignant nor amused. She felt detached from the whole situation, partly because of her physical position.

She sat with her head resting on the chairback. The upward angle of her vision abolished Penstone and veranda and the ground itself, showing only a star-speckled area of night sky framed between two fluted columns. She'd stretched out her legs and crossed her ankles. She was vaguely aware that her body in that position had an unresisting look. And she actually felt somehow inert, passive.

He had stopped speaking. Though Nikki remained motionless, watching the sky, she was acutely aware of him, silent there in the dark, a stealthy, rapacious jungle creature. She shifted her eyes toward him. He was just sitting there staring at her. The strength of his desire was almost a tangible force.

"Don't say no," he said again. His voice, low and hoarse, had a rough tone, like . . . like a bruising caress.

"All right," she said faintly. "But go away, I'm tired."

"Going," he agreed quickly, getting to his feet. He moved around to the side of her chair. "Good night."

When she neither spoke nor stirred, he bent and kissed her cheek. She pushed him away sharply. He backed off at once, apologizing. "Sorry . . . Going . . . Right away."

When he drove off, Nikki got up lazily and dawdled toward the steps as if going down to the yard. Instead she spun and ran to the door shouting, "Eavesdroppers!"

She could hear the maid and the cook hustling through the house and streaked after them. They beat her to the kitchen by a half-second.

"Gotcha!" she cried, bursting in.

The cook, still puffing, gave her a look of massive innocence.

"No, you didn't."

"I did, too."

"Did not."

Then, simultaneously, the three of them broke into laughter.

"I never saw anything like it," the cook cried, collapsing in laughter on a chair. "Running foot races with the lady of the house!"

"You've got to be in training to work around here," Nikki said. "How long were you snooping? I bet you got there before he did."

"You think we were going to *miss* something?"

"You're terrible!" Nikki laughed. "I'm mad at you."

"Why, honey, don't feel that way. I'll tell you real dirt about him. And a girl that was drunk and riding around with him while you were gone."

"Not interested," she said, starting out of the room.

"If it should ever get back to somebody you like very, very much," the cook's voice followed her, "there would be trouble. Because the girl is his wife."

Nikki turned, came back and sat down at the table and stared across at the cook.

"Who?"

"The young judge's wife."

"No!" Nikki exclaimed. "Vic Hollister's wife and Penstone? Are you sure?"

The cook nodded solemnly several times, then launched into the specific details of who had seen them, where and when, at a time Vic was in Norfolk.

". . . nothing but a tramp and never was. She's got soused and picked up men in taverns and roadhouses before; you've heard about it. And maybe you heard about her with Penstone, too. It's been whispered around before. Only it never was so sure and open and seen by so many as this time. Why, it's a scandal. If the young judge shoots the both of them dead, I just wish I could get on the jury that sets him free."

Nikki listened, bright-eyed. She pried and probed avidly for every detail she could get. Not about Penstone and Vic's wife, but about Vic's marriage *in toto*.

By the time Nikki turned in for bed she had found out shocking things. Shocking but believable, even though admittedly she was eager to believe the worst of that bitch. She evidently was, and had been, the kind of wife who deprived her husband of rightful sexual satisfaction as a matter of policy.

The outrageous slut, Nikki fumed. She wished she could kill her! To have a woman like that happen to one of the very finest men alive was monstrous.

She was too badly upset about it to sleep. She paced, brittle with tension, the back of her neck rigid. How awful for Vic. She couldn't stand it. *Vic* subjected to such a life. A woman like that jeopardized his professional position and violated his dignity and pride and ate away his sense of manhood and worth. She must, inevitably, undermine and corrode the finer elements of his nature.

Vic, oh, dearest, dearest Vic! she thought, tears burning her eyes, *how dreadful for you. It breaks my heart.* She sat on the bed in the dark wiping her eyes and feeling his misery and pain.

She could not ease herself. She had to sleep, she knew, but she couldn't. It did no good to try to relax when she was so glad—she meant *sad*. What a preposterous mistake!

She sat scowling for several minutes, then admitted it. Of course she was glad. Glad that that marriage was doomed and might shatter at any minute.

In fact, the thought was luscious! She fairly licked her lips. She lay down smiling and stretched out luxuriously and relaxed. And she slept deeply, sweet-dreaming about dancing with Vic and running up and down stairs with Vic and flying with Vic. . . .

But when she woke and got up in the morning, there was no dancing or flying in her mood. She trudged. Her face was gloomy. Gloomy with virtue, she thought, unamused. Because Vic had a marriage. She'd almost shattered her best friend Dolores' marriage. She had resolved never again to be in the least way responsible for such a thing. So she couldn't give Vic the love he needed.

Chapter Nine

At noon she was in the county seat, about to go into the bank with a deposit, when she saw Vic coming along the walk. She felt a quickening of pleasure, then at once, like a double beat she felt a pang in her breast.

Vic walked leadenly, his gaze downcast, a heavy frown across his protruding brow ridge. The brightness of her yellow-and-blue striped cotton dress caught his eye and repelled it like an aggravating intrusion. His glance flicked away, then back. Seeing who it was, he began to grin. When he moved to her, his step—she was sure she wasn't imagining—was lighter.

"Hello, Vic. How are you?"

"Fine. Slight headache," he said, dismissing it. "So you're home," he said approvingly, and continued in a teasing affectionate voice. "And rushing the season in that summer dress. Just to show off your arms. Aren't you chilly?"

"No. Yes," she admitted, laughing at herself.

He was standing closer to her than he usually did. He lifted his hand and fit it to the slim rounding of her bare upper arm. He stroked very lightly, then squeezed briefly in one of those rare gestures of possessiveness. She looked at him meltingly. The precious touch lasted no more than three or four seconds, then his hand fell away, but she continued to feel its warm imprint. Her craving for him was so strong she knew it must show nakedly in her eyes. She looked away.

"Going to the bank?" Vic said matter-of-factly.

"Yes." She looked down, opening her purse. "Deposits. Checks from the dairy and on the produce from my greenhouses. Look." She gave him checks, bankbook, deposit slips. "Isn't that good, Vic?"

"Helps," he said, nodding and beginning to go through the checks. His hands trembled slightly. His eyes, she noted unhappily, those fine, deep, intelligent eyes, were bloodshot. She was looking at him worriedly and scraping at her underlip with her teeth when he glanced at her, catching her. He laughed humorlessly. "I look like hell, don't I?"

She nodded.

"Thanks," he muttered, frowning. He returned his attention to her deposit slip. She realized he was checking her addition.

"Honestly, Vic, I *can* be trusted to *add* correctly."

"True." he handed the papers back to her. "I suppose it props my ego to try thinking of you as still the little girl, hopelessly young and small and below me, looking up," he said lightly enough, but there was a bitterness around his mouth.

She spoke hurriedly.

"I *am* still small and below and looking up to you, Vic. And I didn't mean to hurt your feelings by agreeing that you look like hell. You don't; you know good and well you couldn't to me. Don't you know?" she pleaded, smiling insistently. "Sure you do. It's just the inflamed, tired look of your eyes that makes me worry that you're working too hard."

"Not work. Hangover," he said disgustedly. "I shouldn't have been so touchy. I suppose you want to get that deposit made. Were you coming up to the office?" She caught the hopeful note.

"If you want me to," she offered, as reluctant as he was to break away.

"Or—say, they're having a pretty fair lunch over at the hotel today. Want to eat with me?"

"Well," she hesitated. "Let me get this deposit made. Wait."

As she walked away from Vic she felt breathlessly excited by the prospect of lunch with him, even in that unromantic old dining room surrounded by scores of people they both knew. When she returned to him, she knew they mustn't risk even that much of a personal social relationship.

"It wouldn't be exactly business," she said dully. "So we'd better not. It's too easy for me to think too personally about you, Vic."

"I understand that. Fact is I was thinking of it as a date, too. But after lunch, come on up. The office is dry, dull and safe. O.K.?"

When she entered his front office, he was lounged back, smoking. They smiled at one another. She took a chair across from him.

"Tell me about the play, Nikki."

"You were right, Vic. I shouldn't have got into it. Because I'm me. I have some sort of lust for chaos. Whatever's orderly and in balance I want to disorganize. I'm destructive. I—"

"Wait! You attack what you have good reasons to suspect are false fronts. You're looking for something worth looking for, Nikki. Truth. About people. Institutions. Whatever. But why did you get things in a wrangle in New York? Don't you believe in that play?"

"Maybe that's it." She shrugged nervously. "Anyhow,

both Kris Drake and Anton Bromley want me. They're already at loggerheads for professional reasons. I tortured them with jealousy over me. I got them in a state where they can't endure one another. And they have to be able to endure one another. In three days the play's opening in Philadelphia. I don't dare go there. I might spark off an explosion."

He sat forward, his face dark with concern. "You sure it's that bad?" he said softly.

She felt choked. She couldn't speak. She just nodded. He reached out his hand and she extended hers to be held.

"I watched the rehearsals on the stage for three days in a row. Anton told me that before I came Kris had got hold of the role. Carried the play. But there was no evidence of it at all in his performances after I came. The two of them spend half their rehearsal time shouting at each other. Having tantrums like children!" She shuddered.

"It's an intensely emotional sort of business. These are all people of temperament, Nikki. It's traditional that they become more and more frenzied as actual opening time approaches. I've been reading about that whole world ever since you got in it."

'You have? And you think I may be overemotionalizing?"

"Scared is a simpler word." He gripped her hand, then released it and sat back.

She sat back and sighed. "Oh, Vic, what did you let me get into all this for?"

"I fought you, Nikki. Even Bromley tried to ease you off."

"Oh, *that!*" She gestured impatiently. "What do I care about Bromley or Drake or that play or the money. I mean *why,* Vic, after my mother's and father's funeral, why didn't you love me enough? Enough to *force* me to marry you. You *knew* I loved you."

He just stared momentarily, then said in a hushed voice, "Past tense?"

"You know the answer to that damned well!"

He came around the desk, drew a chair alongside hers and sat gripping her hands and looking almost grimly into her eyes.

"I love you, too, Nikki," he said, barely aloud.

"Don't say that. It's too late to say that."

"You've heard the rumors about my marriage, the same as everybody else. They're true. I've got the *rottenest* life. Nikki. I don't know where to turn. Here I am a young man with a career I should be enjoying and a big future that I should be thinking about. But do you know which direction I dream? Backward. I reminisce like a man my father's age. I remember about you and me and how good it was, and I wish I were living back in that time."

"Vic, that's terrible, yearning for the past that way. You always had good, solid, level-headed plans, and a *future*," she said, looking at him anxiously. "Vic, honey, you really worry me."

"How I got into it, I don't know. How it's developed to this stage is too sordid to go into. Whose fault it is I can't say . . . for sure."

"It's not yours, Vic," she said fiercely. "And don't you start thinking it is. Hear?"

"Thank you for saying that, Nikki. To hear it from you is very, very good. An insidious thing happens when you get in a fix like I'm in. I can't see working for a future that might benefit *her*. That's damned insidious, isn't it?" He smiled sourly, got up and went around the desk to his own chair. "When a man is betrayed by a woman, the question of his manhood comes up. Even, probably, in your mind, Nikki."

"Never."

"Still, in your time *you* rejected me. Remember? Some doubt existed in your mind about me, some suspicion of inadequacy, deficiency."

"It wasn't that, Vic. I wasn't in any emotional condition to judge."

"Except that, as much as you needed protection and strength, you refused mine. Well, I'm just musing. Wondering. Calling myself before the bench. Heavy stuff. If I want to drive you off as my friend, even as my client. I'm doing a very good job of it. . . . Nikki, if I should drop out on a purely social call, would I get in?"

"Of course. Downstairs. Not because I have any question about your adequacy as a man and a lover, understand. It's just that I have a rule I'm scared to break, Vic; I can't have anything like that to do with a married man. In your case I'm sorry about it. Very sorry, Vic, believe me. But . . ." She gestured futilely.

After all, she thought at home that night, he was continuing to live with the woman. If he was honoring that marriage, she had a perfect right to stick by her resolution, however stupid it was, considering the nature of that destructive marriage.

While she was having dinner two nights later, Anton Bromley phoned from Philadelphia. He was very calm and glum, filling her in on the emotional state of the company as a whole. He droned on about hotel accommodations, the safe arrival of costumes and scenery and props.

"You sound depressed, Anton."

"I want you here. You could still be here in plenty of time for the opening tomorrow night. I miss you Nikki."

"I'm too busy here, Anton. I couldn't do anybody there any good. I'll send telegrams to everybody."

"Say you love me, Nikki."

She frowned at the phone, remaining silent. She took a breath. "All right, Anton. I love you. Phone me after the performance . . . O.K.?"

"Yes. Listen, Kris is going to call you. You'd better assure him that you're his, all his, just saving yourself in purity for him. Tell him it's true and eternal love you've got for him. Will you?"

"I hate this damned duplicity. But, yes, I will. Bye. I've got to ring off. Someone just came."

"A man?"

"It's business," she said testily. "Now, good-bye, Anton. Of course, I wish you the very best of luck."

She hung up. The maid had just let Vic in. Nikki had no sooner greeted him and walked hand in hand into the second parlor with him when the phone rang again. It was Kris.

"Nikki, I want to ask you a simple question. Mrs. Reed said you fired her because she was going to tell me about a man down there who broke in on you and made love to you."

"I fired her because I don't need her. And because I know she was your spy. And because she's too close to a bull for my tastes. And no man has made love to me, *since* . . . well, you know when. Is that all you had to talk about? Is that why you called long distance on the eve of the opening of that play, to plague me with things like that?" she demanded.

The sharp flick of her tongue started him apologizing profusely. She cut into his abject flow of words.

"Kris, I want to tell you something. I expect you to get up there tomorrow night and take the stage. Not just walk through that part. But carry it the way I know you can. I know why you were fouling up while I was in New York. It was to antagonize Anton. You think I admire him. Well, I am asking one thing of him: to return me a profit on my investment. That's his meaning to me. Just remember, Kris, that there'll be only one reason you might fail: to keep *Anton* from having a hit. Do you realize you might want that, and cut off your nose to spite your face?"

"That's it. That's it," he said excitedly. "That's the only reason I ever did badly. Why, this role's a walk-through. I couldn't possibly miss, except if I didn't realize I was trying to cut off my nose to spite him. But for *you*, Nikki, I'll see to it that I don't cut it off. I promise. Because I love you. All I need is to hear that you still love me. And are still *my* girl."

"You know I am. And you know I love you."

Vic had drifted in. He stood looking at her in disbelief. By the time she had hung up, he looked miserable.

"It was a lie, Vic. I swear it. I had to do it. Anton called me and made it absolutely clear that Kris had to have that assurance. Among the people in that world the word 'love' has no more meaning than I don't know what. Don't look at me that way, Vic," she begged.

"To *you* the word has meaning though," he said. He stepped close and put his hands on her waist and looked down at her. "When you counterfeit it! *Hell*, Nikki, that's not you!"

She put her arms around him and held him tightly, pressing her cheek on his chest. "Oh, Vic darling! I don't know *what* I am any more." She held him tighter and shut her eyes. "I was dreaming backward today, too. Just like you do. I wish . . . I wish, Vic, that we were, both of us, back there right now. And could stay there!"

114

He patted and stroked her body and held her in his arms, resting his face against her head. The bond with him was so strong and good and solid, she thought, blissfully. He was so fine, so unhappy; he needed her love as she needed his.

She heard the car, felt him lift his head.

"Whose car is that?" he said, peering out the window.

Nikki opened her eyes, frowning, and looked outside.

"Oh, Lord! Penstone!"

"That son of a bitch!" Vic's face became flinty. "I'm not sure—not yet—if he's the current back-door husband at my house. But I *am* damned sure he's not going to come around *here* bothering *you!*"

Vic started to move.

"Wait. Wait, please." She clutched his sleeve. "I'll send him away."

"I'll send him!"

Vic shook her off and walked to the door, rolling his shoulders. He went outside, made a militant right turn and strode briskly down the veranda. Nikki followed him out, trailing by two or three paces. Penstone had left his car and crossed the drive. He was climbing the end steps to the veranda. Nikki spurted to catch up with Vic. He raised his arm to the side like a semaphor, blocking her.

"Please, Vic." She clutched his upper arm in both hands and tugged. It was unyielding. "Don't lose your head. I can handle him."

"Stay out of it." His voice had deepened.

The commanding sound, the aggressive sight of him gave her a quick, sharp thrill. Through his shirt and jacket she could feel the bands and bulges of taut, hard male muscle, vibrant with dangerous power. She had a sense of the delicacy of her slender hands and fingers against him, a knowledge of her feminine softness and smallness and the futility of protesting whatever his maleness willed.

Currents of sensation raced through her body, tingled hotly in the flesh of her breasts and belly, and filled her with sudden fierce pleasure. An instant later she was ashamed and afraid.

Penstone had come a dozen feet down the veranda.

He began to stare. His pace slowed and Nikki detected a beginning swagger. He came to a wary stop just beyond the table and chair set of outdoor furniture.

Light from the line of windows showed him in hat, suit, tie, shined shoes. He carried a flat, oblong gift package. He shifted the package from one hand to the other, a scowl gathering on his face. Shorter and heavier than Vic, he was part blubber—but so were those immense, formidable Japanese wrestlers. Unquestionably he was strong and mean, and a stomper, a rock-and-broken-bottle alley fighter and brawler.

Nikki ran out and around Vic, stopped a few feet from Penstone, facing him.

"You'd better go," she said urgently.

His glance flicked to her, to Vic, back to her.

"What is this?" he said gruffly.

"It's going to start out," Vic called, "as a request to leave. She doesn't want you around here."

"What's it to him?" Penstone snorted.

"Now the request," Vic said, "becomes an order!"

Nikki turned to face Vic. She shook her head vigorously. He just stood, expressionless, looking past her. Abruptly there was a thudding-thrumming sound behind her that made her jerk around. Penstone had thrown the package on the metal table. He pointed to it.

"I brought you a present. A book. A first-class book! He think he can chase me off? He think he's man enough?"

"Yeah!" Vic answered.

Nikki positioned herself between them, facing the house.

"This is silly. There's no reason for this." She kept looking across one shoulder, then the other. "I don't want this. I want you both to just calm down and. . . ."

She was standing with her bare, sandaled feet apart, nervously swaying her hips a little from side to side, causing her thin, knee-tickler skirt to swing. She was conscious of moving her toes delicately so that the bright red nail polish twinkled. Penstone's gaze dropped to her feet and bare spread legs for a lecherous moment. Vic saw it. His face flushed.

Vic suddenly ripped off his jacket and flung it to the

yard. Penstone threw his hat down and began a heaving motion, getting his thick shoulders out of his own jacket. He backed off, hurrying to get the coat off as Vic started for him.

"No," Nikki said.

She was aware of the limpness of her protest. Her whole effort had been tepid, she knew. As capable as she was of asserting her will with angry force and determination, she had not done it. She had let this build and intensify beyond any stopping point. Her heart was hammering. She was hot all over. Her mouth was dry. She was breathless. Her eyes glittered. She was afraid. But she wanted to know—*didn't* want to know—if Vic lacked a winning punch. If there was a fatal "will to defeat" in him. She was scared to know, but she *must* know!

Penstone was out of his coat and off the veranda. Vic leaped at him, throwing a punch. Penstone ducked under it. He squatted, then seemed to catapult upward. Nikki winced as he threw two fistfuls of gravel at Vic's face. He hopped backward, went into a deep crouch, his feet widely spread. An instant later he came up and forward, and butted Vic's stomach with the driving weight of his whole body back of his hard thick head. The blow drove Vic backwards, his arms flailing for balance.

Nikki held her breath. She wanted to scream a warning as Penstone crouched and sprang in another butting rush, but there was no time. Vic twisted and caught the impact on one hip. He leaped aside and in a lightning-fast maneuver circled and brought both fists clubbing down on the back of Penstone's exposed neck.

Penstone sprawled, belly down in the gravel, letting out a single grunt. He rolled, shielding his head with one arm, his groin with the other. A gentleman fighter, Vic didn't stomp or kick, but stood off, fists doubled, his body semi-crouched and jogging up and down. Nikki's head ached. She wanted to scream, *Damn it, you're not up against a gentleman fighter!*

When Penstone was up, Vic went at him, his fists smashing, cutting, slashing; in crosses, combinations and hooks. Penstone tried to punch and slug and keep out of the way of the blows. Vic was battering his face.

They moved like a grisly dance team, past the end of the veranda onto the lawn, Penstone retreating, Vic driving, pounding.

Penstone's nose was bleeding. A few smashing blows later there was a cut over his eyes and a red, gory stain over half his cheek. Vic shifted to body punches, doubling Penstone forward. He chopped at his head and stomach alternately. Penstone looked wobbly. Vic saw his condition, took aim and delivered a solid blow that knocked him down. He just lay there, then sat resting, breathing heavily.

Vic looked down and said, "Ready to go home?"

"Yeah."

Nikki took a great breath, grinned and blinked back tears of relief.

But Penstone got up and tried to slug Vic. Vic set about whipping him again. Then Penstone gave an injured bellow and mashed himself to Vic, catching him in a bear hug and immobilizing his arms. Nikki could see his knee driving up like a piston at Vic's groin. In a sickening flash they had both fallen to the ground, with Vic on his back.

Penstone dove away, both arms reaching. His hands seized one of the whitewashed stones lining a flower bed. He turned, moved at a crawl toward Vic, the grapefruit-sized stone raised. He smashed it down murderously; directly toward Vic's head. Had it hit the target, it could have crushed Vic's skull. Vic fended off the first blow, trying to roll; he fended off the second. The third grazed him. After a moment the whole side of his face oozed blood.

Penstone got to his feet and began to kick with all his might at Vic's back. He prepared to leap on Vic with both feet. Vic got away and upright. But he kept shaking his head, wiping at the blood on his face. Obviously he was a little stunned.

The two men stood panting and bloody, watching each other savagely. Penstone rushed, throwing a wide, looping roundhouse blow that Vic barely managed to deflect. Another punch drove straight into Vic's stomach. Vic maneuvered, backed and weaved, trying to stall and recover, throwing punches that had no more than nuisance effect.

Win, Vic, Nikki thought passionately, *beat him, beat him, please, darling.*

The maid and the cook had come to the door and were watching in horror. Vic was clearly taking the worst of it. She *had* to stop it now. Yet, she couldn't bring herself to interfere. This brute must not win. But the decision wasn't hers to make. She had no right to change events. To falsify the reality, the truth, even if it proved to be ugly, unbearable truth.

A horrid fantasy swept her. She could see him triumphant, this bloody, ugly Neanderthal, this apostle of brute force. He would come, unopposed, and would seize his prize. If she resisted, he would smash her to the ground. Rip off her clothes. Attack and use her naked body. Force her flesh to receive his ugly animal body.

To be mastered and made the mate, the spoils of such a conqueror would be death. A destruction of every value and meaning. Against the sickening force of that deathly idea the life force rose, hot and throbbing in her womb. There was an intense sexual fire through her whole body that made her dizzy. She clamped her thighs together, fighting back the ugly, orgiastic flood of feeling. She shut her eyes to keep from seeing the dreadful fight, but she couldn't stop herself from looking.

And Vic was stronger. He had held on. He had rallied. He had again taken command of the fight!

It went on and on. They slugged and punched and backed and filled until their arms were leaden. They were inflicting less and less damage. Neither of them was losing or winning. Both were receptive when she rushed at them and screamed almost hysterically for them to stop ... *stop* ... STOP.

They walked away from each other.

"I'll get you," Penstone grumbled. "You just wait."

"You want some more?" Vic demanded.

"*Stop it!*" Nikki ordered.

Penstone went to his car, muttering threats.

"What did you say?" Vic raged at the top of his voice. "*I'll get you!*"

"You loud-mouth back-door husband! If I ever confirm some filthy gossip about you and my wife, Penstone; if you ever violate the honor of my house, you son-of-a-bitch, I'll come gunning."

"Yeh . . . Yah . . . !" Penstone stood by his car, wiping blood off his face. Then he managed a loud, coarse laugh, got quickly in the car and dove off.

Nikki had to fight Vic to keep him from following.

Chapter Ten

"I did it, a shabby thing, but I finally did it," Vic said, the next night. "Put a detective on her. She claims she's playing cards tonight. She may be, because she suspects I'm watching her. And Penstone knows I mean it; I'll gun him."

He'd been pacing up and down the music room. Nikki, sitting huddled in an armchair in a flowered housecoat, listened receptively, watching him nervously. His face was puffy, one eye was discolored, bruise marks showed on his jaw and there was a rectangular patch of white adhesive on his cheek.

There was an angry snap to his eyes and that protruding brow ridge had a particularly menacing look. He carried his head forward aggressively, his broad-based neck arching. The fight clearly had not slaked his belligerence, but roused it more intensely. She was proud of his spirit but it filled her with anxiety and a sort of chill foreboding.

He stopped in front of her chair and looked down at her with a quizzical frown as if she had questioned him critically.

"You are, of course, jeering inwardly, asking why all the melodrama, the meaningless histrionics. How empty can I get, protecting a home that's not a home, threatening to kill a man for the sake of a woman I don't love and who doesn't love me!"

"You misunderstand me completely," Nikki said meekly, lowering her gaze, "if you can think I'm jeering inwardly. Or that I'm against you in any way." She gazed up with wide, love-filled eyes.

He turned his back and walked over to the grand

piano and walked his fingers along the keyboard, plinking the out-of-tune strings in an aimless pattern. He sat on the bench, facing her.

"It's you I love." He got up. "You can't help but see the preposterousness. There's something musty and false in the whole idea. Conforming to a dead tradition that I never lived by—not to any great extent. It's romanticism. You see it, but you're mum. Uninvolved. Unconcerned."

"No."

"Of course your mind is on—" he glanced at his watch— "Act III of *The Garden of Weeds*, as it unfolds itself magically, with the star-luster of the sequin-toothed pretty boy in Philadelphia. What happens on that stage is reality to you."

"You're making me miserable," she suddenly wailed. "You know how important you are to me. You know I'm worried sick about this mood of yours. I'm trying to be a woman and feminine instead of belligerent and aggressive and you jump on me about it!"

He sighed and left the room, calling back, "I'm getting another drink."

"Bring me one," she yelled.

He came back with his own whisky and soda, nothing for her.

"You really shouldn't drink. No woman should."

"Don't judge everybody by that drunken wife of yours," she said nastily and regretted it at once. "I didn't mean to say that!"

"What the hell, it's what you mean. I'd rather hear you say something than nothing all the time. What's all this passive willingness about you?" He pulled a chair to hers, sat and leaned close. "Honey, don't lose your self-confidence; that's what's happening to you."

"I'm going to get drubbed, Vic, I just know it. How am I going to pay that note on time next month?" Her mouth quivered. "I'm going to sell every piece of jewelry I've got when I go to New York next time. Stuff that's been in the family for—well, it doesn't matter. They said they'd give forty thousand. But we're still going to be short. And now this with Penstone—that bank's liable to call the whole thing in. I should have gone to the Richmond bank as I threatened to do.

And if the play doesn't go. . ." She broke off, stared at him, shaking her head. "You told me and told me!"

"Well, we'll be able to stall. Your crops are coming along. There's a certain small income till then. And I tell you, that play's just liable to make it. Yes, it is. Don't get scared!"

"But *this property's* the collateral at Penstone's bank. You know that, Vic. Can he finagle and seize it? That's all he's ever wanted, my land. He even asked me to marry him, to combine our holdings, he's so land-crazy!"

"He *what*? Penstone had the gall to ask *you* to marry *him*?"

"Just a few nights ago. He begged me not to say no yet, but think it over a while, And. . ." Ashamed, she averted her eyes. "I *was* thinking it over. Thinking that maybe it was a kind of fate, an inevitability, a sort of poetic justice. My great-great-grandfather was his kind of man, on a bigger, brainier scale. I thought, after all I'm only a woman, nature demands a certain role for a woman. I've been violating that role. And coming to grief doing it, Vic. Oh, don't look at me. It's true, I was considering it. A woman doesn't look for aesthetics in a male—just strength enough to protect her."

"Shut up," he said in a low, hoarse voice. "Nikki, you're desperate." He sat on her chair, pressed close to her. He took her face in both his hands. She closed her eyes and he kissed them. He kissed her cheeks and her lips, very lightly. "You're a fine girl, Nikki, a lovely, wonderful girl. I don't want to hear you thinking like that. It sullies you."

She couldn't help giggling. "*Sullies*. Aren't you quaint, you darling! Ah, but you make me feel so good. You're wonderful for me. And please promise me one thing. Forget that gun stuff!"

"Nikki, this is one thing I thought you, more than anyone, would understand!"

"You yourself said it's empty. You don't live by that tradition. That home isn't precious to you. Why play a romantic, meaningless game?"

"It's not the home, or the tradition or the woman— God knows it's not her! It's *me*, Nikki. My pride, my dignity, my honor. An insult to my manhood is involved. It's pride, not false pride, but gut-deep!"

"But primitive. You, of all people, are past that. The rule of law, you used to pontificate, without which no civilization ... Vic, you know I don't give a damn if you'd kill him. I'd be glad! But it won't do you any good. Not in this day and age. A sound, solid lawyer doesn't lose his head! Or rather, his belief in reason and law. It would hurt you, destroy confidence in you among clients. Afterward, you couldn't explain it to yourself why you'd abandoned your whole meaning, Vic. A fist fight, all right; even a bloody, crippling affair. But a gun? Think, Vic."

"When I think, fine. I understand it all. Having you say it helps. I'll try to stay balanced. But sometimes the deadly insult involved enrages me. Not hotly—coldly. I could—well, I won't! Nikki, I need you. We're for each other. All the way!"

"Please don't ask me, Vic. Don't please. I can't stand refusing you. But *I have to*. I can't get over what I did to somebody. I can't touch a marriage and help break it. That's all."

The phone rang. They both got up and hurried to it.

"Must be Anton," she said breathlessly. Vic nodded. She reached for the handset and Vic's hand at the same time. She squeezed his hand and said: "Nikki Duquesne speaking." Her eyes widened. "It's him," she whispered to Vic. "Yes ... Really? ... It did ...?" A smile began to spread over her face, and the contagion of it touched Vic, then he winced and touched his bruised jaw.

Anton's words came torrentially, and they were singing, laughing, exclamatory words. Whenever he gave her a chance she put in excited comments. "Yes, put him on, to .... Kris," she whispered to Vic.

It was fifteen minutes before she hung up. She picked up the skirt of her housecoat and performed a small dance, then hugged Vic. Then they both went in and had a drink.

The celebration was a trifle premature. Anton's call next morning included reviews. Only the *Inquirer* had given the show a really favorable review. Another was a shrug, a third was a blistering pan. However, Anton was not too depressed. He spoke of plunging into rewrites and a general revamping of certain weak parts and rang off in a fairly cheerful mood.

Vic arrived unexpectedly in midafternoon. He found her in the apple orchard. She knew from his face that something had happened.

"They met in a motel this morning. Spent an hour. Went separate ways. Where she is now, I don't know. I'll find her in a tavern, no doubt. And get her home. I'll tend to her. Then . . . I can't help it, Nikki, I'm going to kill him."

She pleaded. She couldn't reach him. He was ice.

The minute he left to look for his wife Nikki went to Penstone's farm. It was the first time she'd ever been there. He wasn't around. He wasn't at the county seat either. When she drove back home, she slowed at his place, and turned in. His car was there.

As she approached the squarish old two-story frame house, he came to the door. He stepped out on the porch. His face was far more battered than Vic's. He stood looking at her malevolently.

"What do you want?"

"Vic knows about this morning."

"So what?"

"He meant it about gunning you. I'll try to stop him, but I'm not sure I can. You'd be smart to lay low and leave his woman strictly alone."

"I'll take her any time I get the itch," he said contemptuously. "I'll show the Hollisters and the Duquesnes what they amount to. I'll either take his woman or the one he's sniffin' around—*you*. You decide which one I'm gonna use at my pleasure. You or her. I'll dump her quick to get it from you, on demand. And the marriage hook don't go with it no more. You lost your chance there. How do you say, Missy?"

She turned and went to her car.

"Want to swap places in the bed with his woman? Maybe you already done that with the front-door husband. What do you say, Missy?"

"You're loathsome."

"You wait, when it comes to loathsome, George ain't started. You know that note you got down at our bank . . . due pretty quick, y'know. Seventy-two thousand dollars. We ain't renewing a nickel of it. I promise you. And wait—don't go off with your cute tail swishin'— wait. The financial report I'm going to see to it that goes out on you, Missy, is going to kill you dead at any other bank. I promise you. And you think Hollister can bail you out? He don't own nothin' except in joint holding with *my* woman. Don't go 'way mad, now, little Missy. And you just tell him if he wants to come with his gun, I got a gun, too."

He had followed her to her car, pounding at her. Driving away, she was pale and her heart was beating so hard it vibrated her whole chest wall.

She didn't know how she got through that day or the next or the next.

Work took Vic to Richmond but he was back every night. And he saw her every night, and often phoned in the middle of the day. He was on and off the idea of using a gun. He didn't know what to do about his wife. Athough he tried to make light of Penstone's threats to ruin her credit, he was worried. In fact he was close to being desperate and so was she.

Vic did not ask again to make love to her, but his need and craving were nakedly obvious. She despised herself for holding to the empty vow when this marriage was one that not only gave nothing, but was destroying a good man. And yet she couldn't bring herself to take him as her lover.

It was four o'clock in the morning when Anton phoned long distance.

"Nikki, you've got to get here at once! Kris is going to walk out. He can do it, too. He's got an escape clause in his contract. You've got to stop him or we're ruined. We've had a good week, making expenses, maybe a couple of thousand more. And the advance sales for New York have been coming along very nicely, over thirty thousand. But a lot of it's sold on his name—let's face that ugly fact. He can't be replaced at this stage. We'd have to refund everything and close up shop. Well, baby, you've just got to get in here and pitch. Everything's so important to you down there in the sticks. But this is *one* time—"

"I'm coming, Anton. Don't get hysterical."

"When?"

"The first plane I can get. Good-bye."

She just sat there shaking and staring. She'd never done it before, but she phoned Vic's house. If that bitch answered, she'd scream. The phone rang and rang. Finally Vic answered.

She poured it all out to him.

"Hold on, I'm coming right away. I'll go with you."

"Oh, would you, darling? I need you so much."

When he got there she was calmer. They had breakfast together. He had too much work to do here to go flying off; she knew it. And so did he.

It was finally agreed he shouldn't go. But she adored him for his offer. In a certain sense he did go with her as a solid inner strength. And she needed it. Because Anton and Kris were at war.

The flight had been smooth; she was no stranger to Philadelphia. And the midday sky here, she thought as the cab took her through Rittenhouse Square, was as sunny as Richmond's. So she had no problem of physical adjustment.

Yet she felt a kind of emotional incoherence. She saw the play's title and Kris' name, spelled out on one end of the Guild Theater's unlit marquee, and the title and his name repeated, plus the leading lady's on the marquee's long front, and she knew the significance of it to herself. But she couldn't connect it to her *self*.

She left the cab and went toward the theater, staring blankly at the bold posters on wallboards and on houseboards within the open outer lobby. The poster design, in orange-black-green was impressionistic, and subtly distorted, featuring a caricature of Kris that gave his handsome smile a sinister twist. It captured the characterization of his role, slandered his Hollywood image and might or might not be true of Kris himself. He didn't know for sure who he was. Which, she thought, gives us a bond.

She visualized herself as a traveler on a detour while she walked back to the stage door, a slim figure in a pastel linen suit and small hat, carrying two light suitcases, her pump heels ticking, a bright, roll puff of red hair bouncing against the pale nape of her neck.

She was expected. The watchman led her across a section of the vast backstage, dim now and quiet as a warehouse, toward the lighted stage. She recognized the stage manager going over lighting cues with an electrician at the big control panel, and, in the wings on the far side of the stage was the production manager, two walk-on players who doubled as understudies, the press agent and two people she didn't know. The cast of eleven was scattered along the lip and sides of the stage watching the leading and second leading ladies in a scene with Anton, who was reading Kris' lines.

Nikki stood in the wings as unobtrusively as possible, but couldn't help peering out into the auditorium, hoping in vain to see Kris. The scene Anton was reading to the girls, one dark and stylish like a chic gypsy, the other a peppery little beauty, took place in the last act and was set in a Brooklyn flat. But ironically, the back curtain, ready for the evening performance, was Scene 1, Act I, and showed a dazzlingly sunlit Mediterranean somewhere on the Riviera.

"Nikki!" Anton cried, spotting her. They moved toward one another. His arms stretched to embrace her, a jaunty grin so like her father's, on his face. "So you're here, darling!"

She held herself tight and turned her face, taking his kiss on her cheek.

"He's not here?" she said impatiently. "Where is he?"

Looking rebuffed, he said, "He's a missing person. He always was; there never was a person inside him."

The rest of the company had begun to gather around. There was a necessary exchange of greetings. Then she frowned at Anton.

"Don't talk riddles. Where is he?"

"Sulking in his tent! Take over," he called to the production manager.

He carried her bags out to the street, bombarded her with questions that she received in a moody silence. He hailed a cab. When it stopped at the hotel within two blocks she said scornfully, "In the 'sticks,' as you call my home, we'd have saved time by walking."

"My baby's in a mean mood. Shall I check you in here?"

"Damn it, I want to get on with what I came for!"

Kris opened the door and smiled wanly. His handsome face looked drained; his eyes were stark. He put his arms around her and held her, or rather held to her like a lost soul. When he moved to kiss her, she couldn't refuse him.

"Now," she said gently, "what's the trouble, Kris?"

"Me," he said dismally. "I'm no good. No damned good."

"That's true," Anton said. Nikki looked at him slashingly. He winked at her. "He's proving he's no good. Right this minute. Yellow-dogging out and stranding a lot of people and ruining a great play and throwing a quarter-million dollars of your money down the sewer. I said he had hopes of talent. He showed he had a little. But no guts. *That* you can't cure!"

Kris went over to the rumpled bed and lay flat on his back.

"That's his answer, flat on his yellow back!"

Kris moaned exhaustedly. "That's his whole repertoire. The reason I can't go on is that I'm worthless. And—"

"The one really rotten review he got he reads over and over like the masochist he is! Well, if he won't do it even for the woman he claims to love, it's hopeless. To hell with it." Anton slammed out of the room.

Nikki stood gazing down at Kris. Then she sat on the edge of the bed. She stroked his forehead. "You're really sick, aren't you, Kris? Well, I know you tried. If you can't, you can't."

She choked up. She turned her face and bit her lip, wanting to cry—for him, for herself, for the simple hopeless pleasure of it.

"I don't know any way to help you. My style's like Anton's, to goad and shame and drive you. It won't work. I don't know what to do. I know you wouldn't quit just to be quitting. Remember, Kris, how you told me what big hopes you had? You wanted so much to do it. It must be crushing for you, too. It just seems so terrible. Wait a minute. . . ." She hurried into the bathroom and sloshed her face with cold water to shock herself out of tears. Finally she felt controlled. She blotted her face and went back to him. He was sitting up, smoking.

"You anyway try to understand me," he said. "But the trouble, you see, is I've got no right to anything. I've had too much gravy. All because nobody really knew how rotten I really am. It took this play to show me. The bastard in that play is no worse than I've wanted to be—and sometimes, partly, was. I'm rotten;

I'm not what I used to try to keep believing I was, It's really a strong, fine play. It deserves a strong, fine actor. You can get one, Nikki. It wouldn't take long."

'It's impossible. I can't last out any more *delays*," she cried. "I'm going broke as it is! Kris, if the play moves you that much, it must be all we hope it is. You're letting your lust for beatings take over your whole life and destroy you. You don't *grasp* this play. The main character isn't all bastard, as you call him!"

"No? Well, then," he said, uncertainly.

"You're clinging to the stupid idea that people are all good or all bad. It's more complex, Kris! You've got to see that about *yourself* and realize you're not damned. I'd rather strip you down and give you a physical whipping than see you choosing this kind of disgraceful beating. Because if you do quit, Kris, you'll never recover from *that* beating you've accepted.

"Now that's all I have to say to you, Kris. Your decision must be yours. I'm checking into this hotel. I'll be in my room all afternoon. You call me if you have anything to say. Otherwise . . ." she shrugged.

"Do you love me?"

"Do I know you?" she countered. She left the room.

He phoned her room in an hour. He was going to be on stage that night.

Nikki was in the audience. For the first time she saw the play whole. She was so tense, so overalert to the audience's reactions, so conscious of Kris Drake, the person attempting to do a job of acting, so conscious of his fellow actors' nervousness about him, so aware of Anton and the author standing at the back of the house, watching with unreadable expressions, that she couldn't possibly have received the play itself.

At the end she made no attempt to judge independently, but simply registered the audience reaction like some applause meter. It seemed sufficient; Anton's congratulations backstage were effusive and deceptive.

He told her tersely that Kris had been better, the rest of the cast worse. She had a midnight supper with Kris. He talked so euphorically about himself and the prospects that she wondered dully if he might be a manic-depressive on the upswing. He literally talked her to sleep. And he was so high that it didn't hurt his feelings; he just laughed indulgently and was easily steered off from trying to make love to her.

She phoned Vic long distance and recounted everything that had happened. Then she pleaded for assurance that he would do nothing rash and when he promised she slept exhaustedly.

She remained till the company ended the Philadelphia engagement. Her function was to hold Kris' hand. He held onto her and he had his fits of depression, but gradually he built confidence. Anton was busier than anyone and worse-tempered. And in that mood he became intolerably domineering.

Late one night in her room, he said, "You're going to have to learn, Nikki, that when you're in my realm, you're to submit to *my* will. That's the first lesson you'll have to learn as an actress."

"I told you, Anton, I'm me. I'm not going to be an actress."

"I've already got a script that's made for you. It's the first thing we work on, once this job's rolling safe. You're a natural actress. There's nothing worse than an actress without a stage. I'm going to shape you into the brightest—"

"That would be an improvement? You propose to improve me? Reshape my life to *your* specifications? Is that how you see our future?"

"Of course. Now quit being coy with me. You've held out past my tolerance. It's time to get your panties off and that cute tail on the bed."

"My! You're so masterful, Anton! You can do whatever you will with me whenever you will it," she said, smiling. "Or so you think."

"C'mon. Don't be a tease. I'm in no mood."

"You know what, Anton?" she said. "The funniest thing. We're suddenly all washed up. I just decided." She walked to the door. "You're finished. You amuse me no more."

"Come off of it, Nikki." He chuckled. "Not just like that."

"Yes. Just like that. It's good-bye."

"This's a pretty tough way to do it!" he protested, his mouth sagging.

"Sorry . . . I'm a pretty tough baby." She opened

the door. When he didn't move, she said sharply, "I told you. You've had it. Now *get out!*"

She gave a farewell dinner for the whole company and saw them entrain for Boston. She bade Kris a very warm good-bye. At the sight of Anton's long face, she relented. She hugged him and whispered, "I'm sorry, darling. But we're still friends."

"That's right." He grinned. "Wish us luck."

"You know! 'Bye . . . 'bye . . ."

She flew home. Vic was at the airport. She rushed into his arms. He gave her a kiss full on the lips and held her very closely.

"God," he said, "I thought you'd never get back!"

"Everything's calm, isn't it?"

"I sent her to Atlanta," he said, his face tightening. "Two days ago. Yesterday, he took off. Left town, for parts unknown. Presumably Atlanta. Well, to hell with it!"

Chapter Eleven

The next weeks were frantic. Both Vic's wife and Penstone reappeared. Vic began to keep an almost day-and-night guard on her. Every time he and Penstone came within sight of one another they glared. The slightest thing, Nikki felt, might trigger off more, and worse, violence. Vic was in regular telephone contact with her, and whenever he could, he came over, or she went to his office.

Then one night he drove onto her property and parked with lights out down by the dairy barn. The dairy foreman phoned her and she drove down. Vic was in sight of Penstone's house, watching road and entrance lane. Nikki slipped into his car beside him. She felt a pistol in his jacket pocket.

"Please, Vic." She got on his lap, put her arms around his neck and gazed into his eyes. "Please let me have that gun!" She pressed close, rubbed her cheek against his and kissed his ear. She whispered, "Vic, I'm freezing inside. What are you doing to me? For *her!* What do you care what she does?"

"I care what that son-of-a-bitch does to me." He set her off his lap. "If he gets her there the minute I'm off guard, it's a deliberate insult, an expression of contempt." He broke off.

A car was coming along the road. It was slowing, then turning into Penstone's lane. Nikki could feel Vic's whole body tense. He was staring.

"It's *her!*" he said icily.

He unlatched his door and started to get out. Hysterically, Nikki pawed out, found the light switch. She turned his headlights on, pinioning the car in Penstone's lane. She began to blast the horn in a frenzied staccato of sound. The car in the lane stopped. It came racing backward to the road. It turned, geared forward and sped away.

Vic swore. He hauled Nikki out of the car. He got in and roared off without a word. He went directly up Penstone's lane.

Nikki was too hysterical to be afraid. She got in her own car and followed him. Vic was banging on the door with his gun. If Penstone was in there, he wasn't coming out.

"He's not here!" Nikki told him.

"His car is. He is. Come out here, you yellow sneak."

"You're not even sure it was *her*," Nikki insisted.

"I know!"

He knew, all right. But the futility of banging on that door soon became clear. He left in his car, Nikki in hers. She thought he'd go home. But he followed to her house. She gave him a drink, but wouldn't speak to him.

Then he said, "I know you're angry with me."

"What a word! *Angry,*" she mocked. "I sure would've been *angry* if you'd got killed. Oh, what an adolescent thrill she must be getting, your beloved wife, to have a gunfighter battling for her. Well, here I am, nowhere. Shut the door when you go, will you? I'm going to bed."

"This did it. Tonight. I'm divorcing her. That's the only way. Will you marry me?"

"That's a good way to end a paragraph. Adds interest."

"I didn't mean to sound casual. I mean it for sure, Nikki."

"An hour ago, I'd have said yes. Yelled it. Now? I don't know. Now, Vic, don't try to kiss me or take me to bed or sway me *that* way. That's unfair. Let me be. I'm too worried about everything to think about anything." She went to the stairs. She came back. She grinned. "I know one thing."

"Such as?" He looked at her adoringly.

"I love you. I love the hell out of you, Vic."

She turned and went to the stairs again.

"Go home. I'm beat."

He laughed and followed her half up the steps and kissed her soundly.

"That was nice. But, please, Vic, go away and let me sleep. See you tomorrow."

"O.K."

"The play's leaving Boston tonight. If it does as well in New Haven. . . ." She crossed her fingers. "Then New York! That's the one that counts."

Nikki made a trip to New York, disposed of her jewelry, sent the certified check to Vic and ran up to New Haven.

The company had quite a number of audiences under its belt and the general mood was high. Kris was holding up fine. He'd got a good personal notice in a Hartford paper. He was eager to make the final jump to the 49th Street Theater for opening night.

"Well," Vic announced casually when she walked into his office the next afternoon. "I just killed George Penstone."

"When's the funeral?" she said, dropping into a chair.

"It was this morning. I decided to revert to adulthood, even though you admire swashbucklers. So I have been talking with some of his fellow directors. I reported his threat to ruin your credit. I pointed out the facts of your financial position. I said we might very well sue a bank if Penstone represented their position. Well, it seems he is no longer a director there."

"You're kidding! No, you're not!" she exclaimed admiringly. "Vic, that's marvelous! I'm so relieved, I can't tell you. Oh, boy, I'm going right over there and get me a loan big enough to—"

"Hold it! I've got all the papers here; the loan's already arranged for all you need. It'll tide you over till fall. If all goes well you're set. We can squeeze you through *even if the play flops!* Assuming your current farming income holds up, and assuming your crops get harvested and to market. How's that suit you, Nikki?"

Chapter Twelve

It was hot in Virginia the night before opening night. Nikki raised her windows to a cooling cross current of air and slipped into bed naked under a sheet. She woke at dawn, realized what day it was. She shivered.

She was lying uncovered on her side, a pillow clamped between her thighs, knees drawn up, the muted orange light of the sun glossing the lovely young feminine contours of her bare back. She rolled on her back, flung away the pillow, and just lay for a while, her knees lifted, one hand resting languidly on her belly.

The light was like dull fire on her exciting body, giving a richness of tone to the fair skin of her breasts, which moved delicately with her breathing. Fully awake, Nikki was aware of a driving, surging, inner rush. She arched and stretched. She sat up. She stood up, trembling on tiptoe. She knew she must hold tight, move slowly. She must pace herself like a race horse or she'd be worn out before the day was over.

By eight-thirty she'd attended to everything she had to concerning the farm. Before nine she was en route to Richmond with plenty of time to make her eleven o'clock flight. Vic, already in Richmond on a court case, had promised to be there to see her off. She counted on a half-hour with him.

He hadn't come at 10:50 when they called her flight. She phoned his Richmond office and exploded when informed he was "out of town." She went out to the gate, fretting, and started across to the plane steps.

"Stop pouting." It was Vic. He caught up, taking her arm.

"Kiss me good-bye *quick*," she demanded.

"No time. Hurry!" He moved her along. "I just checked my bag in. Hustle! I'm coming, too. . . . Climb!"

Following her up, he made her grin and almost giggle by saying in a lecherous undertone, "Get that action! Ooo-la-la, *quelle derrière!*"

Luckily they got seats together. During the in-flight lunch he put his dessert on her tray. She shook her head no; he nodded yes.

"Male courting bird offering delicacies."

"In that case," she said. She tasted and smiled.

When the trays were gone he took her hand.

"Male courting birds also offer bright objects," he said, his tone light, his eyes sober.

She realized with a start that he was slipping a ring on her finger. Third finger, left hand. She gaped at the large square-cut diamond engagement ring. She didn't look at him, not knowing what to say.

Vic laughed. "The dirty bird knows the bright object will hold her attention so he can sneak up on her and have his wicked way. Well, are you glad? Are you happy about it? Are we engaged?"

"Yes. . ." she said faintly. "I think so . . . I . . ."

She turned her face to him, forcing a big smile. Her brilliant green eyes probed him. He was everything, everything to her! But as a lover he was a total stranger. What if—what if—sexually . . .? The thought broke off. She felt a little panicky. "Oh," she tried to put enthusiasm in her voice, "This is so wonderful . . . so . . ." she fumbled, "*thrilling!*"

She found herself straining forward as the cab crossed into Manhattan. It was nearly three. She had a salon appointment at three-thirty. She had to drop Vic at the Plaza at 59th and Fifth, go to her apartment in the Seventies, go down to the salon in the lower fifties. There was just no time for 49th Street. But . . .

"I've just got to see it, Vic," she blurted. "Right now!"

"Go to the 49th Street Theater," Vic told the driver.

"If you want to get checked in," she said, as they waited on a signal across from the Plaza, "and freshen up, it's all right."

"I'm going with you," he said. Firmly.

She looked at the hansoms at the curb beyond the avenue, then pointed at a corner of the park and said irrelevantly, "That's Central Park; Zoo's right there in that corner."

"Fascinating. Especially," he said drily, "to a man who's been here fifty times."

They crossed the avenue. She looked out her window rather regretfully as they passed his hotel, unaware that she was fiddling with the engagement ring till Vic said, "If you want to twist it down and off instead of around and around . . ."

"Nothing like that!" she cried. "But didn't you say she pleaded and promised to be better an—"

"I've heard such pleas and promises too many times," he said flatly.

"But you might pity her again. Give her another chance. That would be human. Understandable. I'm not saying it critically. You might believe in her sincerity this time. And feel obliged to—well, you know—and feel guilty if you didn't."

"What you're driving at is transparent, Nikki. You pity that sequin-toothed weakling. So suddenly you're not sure of the etiquette of being engaged to a still married man. You don't want Kris to see that ring. You'd have taken it off if I weren't here."

Without denying it she said, "I don't expect he'll be there. He'll be resting. I just want to look at the *place*."

"O.K." He squeezed her hand and smiled at her. "Don't be tense."

"And it wouldn't be a matter," she persisted, "of my *personal* interest. Don't imagine he's my lover—or Anton either. That's all past. I swear, Vic. There *was* something, I'll be straight. But past tense. I promise. Still, there's a problem of morale. Opening night and all. His confidence not being too dependable . . ."

"Then he must still be in love with you. Must still have hopes," Vic said tightly. "Obvious. Right?"

The cab swung into 49th Street.

"Look . . . oh, isn't it marvelous, Vic!"

Bright, gleaming banners rose from either end of the marquee to the center top of the building proclaiming A GARDEN OF WEEDS . . . KRIS DRAKE. The cab stopped.

She got out and feasted on the signs and photos, outside and in the outer lobby. Vic came in with her. She grinned, pointed like a conspirator at two lines of people at the box office windows.

"Aren't those ticket buyers beautiful?" she whispered.

She banged on the inner lobby doors. A workman opened almost at once.

"I'm Miss Duquesne. Anybody here? Mr. Bromley? C'mon, Vic," she said, stepping inside and motioning to him. The workman told her there were some people backstage. She drew an exultant breath.

"Feel how cool—the air-conditioning's in fine shape. He was worried." She moved to the head of an aisle, surveyed the rows of empty seats. A small orchestra was rehearsing on the otherwise empty stage.

Nikki walked down the aisle, around to the stage steps. She went up, with Vic close behind her. She went backstage, calling out. There were some stage hands and carpenters in evidence. In a few moments Anton, unshaven, looking haggard, wearing dirty old pants and sweatshirt, came hurrying forward.

"Hi, Nikki. 'Lo there, Hollister. We're up to our ears. The cast's sleeping at their hotels. Be here at six. Your tickets are up at your apartment. Glad you're here. But gotta rush. Million things. That technical problem of getting the orchestra out of the pit after the overture and backstage for the off-scene music when the curtain comes up is still driving me nuts. Short of rewriting, I dunno what . . . So good seeing you both. 'Bye." He walked away, vanished behind the stage.

"We'd better go," Vic said. She agreed.

She was only a trifle late at the salon.

She had planned on either a wide bouffant or a high, intricately formal hair-do to go with that opulent gown with forty yards of rich foamy material in the skirt, or the overelaborate panniered and bustled and flounced affair. Quite abruptly she thought, *Whatever happened, you sybarite, you hedonist, you voluptuary, to your taste for simple uncluttered lines? How about the clear-eyed, self-possessed look?*

She had her hair done almost as starkly as a helmet, drawn tautly back from her temples, and upswept and packed in tight: the no-nonsense, this-is-me look, that featured her alert green eyes and the vital truth of a mind behind them.

Her gown, too, she thought amusedly, asserted a truth—about her figure, following it faithfully. A dark sheath, deceptively plain, its success at showing her figure had been achieved by the artful trickery of skilled and expensive craftswomanship. The moral being, perhaps, that the truth was costly. And if, in Kris' dressing room before the performance, she wore the ring of another man, thus showing him that she was not "with" him all the way . . .

Vic got to her apartment at 7:25, looking splendid in his white tuxedo jacket.

"You're an artwork, Nikki!" he said, smiling broadly. "Simply beautiful. Since the lips are not for smearing . . ." He bent and kissed the round of her shoulder.

Vic looked over at the bar hesitantly. She hurried over and made him a drink. At the last moment she decided on a short one for herself, too.

The street outside the theater was a mob scene at a circus. Fringe banners had been added to the marquee, blazing with lights. At both ends there were big revolving drum arc lights, their pale beams sweeping the twilight sky. The sidewalks for half a block in either direction were dense with people, many of them teen girls.

A swarm of police had set up rope barriers. Cabs and limousines moved at a crawl to the curb space. Everyone emerging from a car was a brief focus of attention. Photographers and society reporters assailed them; friends among ticketholders jamming lobby and walk hailed them. Much of the audience would be professional people from all segments of the theater and press. Including producers "Come to bury me . . ." as Anton said grimly. Show-off men, raucous females, stylish women wearing ornate gowns and fortunes in jewels, drunks, loud-mouth poseurs shouted from group to group in the lobbies.

Nikki and Vic went in, moving slowly through the mass. They went to their fifth-row aisle seats, carrying programs and souvenir books.

"Let's go backstage," she said.

There was backstage noise and confusion, too. She

went along the line of the lower floor dressing rooms, spoke a word to each of the principals. She had sent flowers and telegrams to the whole cast and the author. Vic had stopped to talk to Anton, then the two went out on the stage to look through the peephole into the auditorium. Nikki rapped and walked into Kris's dressing room.

He turned from his dressing table and grinned.

"Guess we can't spoil each other's makeup with a kiss," he said, "but afterward, you darling! You'll be at the party Anton's giving of course?"

She stood leaning back against the door, her left hand out of his view. She looked at him steadily, soberly for several seconds, seeing him in perspective.

"No," she said, finally. She extended her left hand, showing him the ring.

"So *that's* how it is? You mean to tell me you've got a chance with Kris Drake and throw it away?"

"M'm-h'm."

"Then you're a fool."

"Thanks for keeping a dry eye. Otherwise I might have wasted pity on you. Well, good luck. My money's riding on you."

"I could break you just like that by doing a bad show." He snapped his fingers. "But I'm above that."

"That's noble. 'Bye-bye."

Most of the crowd was in their seats before the overture was through, but some were still coming in noisily. She wouldn't have noticed the clumping of the musicians getting from pit to backstage if she hadn't been listening.

And then, at last, the curtain rose.

The first act was riddled by the commotion and talk of noisy, drunken latecomers and by repeated applause from claques. But the cast held on grimly and got through. The second act was quieter. Presently the play began to dominate even that outrageous first-night crowd. Vic went out for each intermission but she didn't budge, having no taste for bucking the crowd.

The last act, with its tightening dramatic scenes, and the musical score barely audible like a muttering, dissonant undertone, held them spellbound, including Vic, she saw, from his intent expression.

The curtain and the stage lights began to lower very, very slowly and then it was done.

The applause was surely more than polite. But there was of course the sense of occasion, the spirit of a party. The whole cast took a bow en masse and individually, the lesser players peeling off one by one, then the principals, and finally Kris took his alone. They brought him back two, three, four times. He beamed. He spotted her and smirked. Nikki shrugged and laughed and nodded and clasped her hands overhead. Then the whole cast again, and author, producer, composer, set designer and eventually almost everybody connected with the production.

The din and the stress of too much response began to scrape her raw. When Vic, loyally beating his hands, said they should go backstage and then to the hotel party, she looked at him levelly and said challengingly, "All right! If *that's* what you want to do."

She just stared at him, anger giving her face a sultry, stormy look. He got the message and he liked it, she saw, feeling a quick, hot little thrill.

From that moment he was a man intent on getting his woman alone. Every obstacle, getting out, getting a cab, getting to her apartment, increased his aggravation. His brow bulged, his voice was rough, and as monosyllabic as possible.

When he got inside her apartment, he locked the door, looking as if he'd slain the last dragon and pulled up the moat. He rolled his shoulders and gave a short laugh. He reached his spread hands and pressed them on the bare skin of her shoulders. He stroked, then pressed, his fingers pulsing against her flesh. He looked at her with wide-open, delighted eyes as if she were something to eat. Then damned if he didn't bury his face against the base of her neck where it sloped into her shoulder, and bite. The pain was sudden and scalding and she slapped him automatically crying, "Ouch, damn you!"

He laughed and yanked her to him and mashed his mouth down on hers, rolling his face, and jabbing his tongue against her lips till she opened. Then he deep-kissed her, driving his tongue in so hard she backed off and broke free. His mouth and hers both were smeared.

"I won't have such roughness. You can't make love to me that way." She kicked off her pumps and walked toward the bedroom, holding herself haughtily erect.

He rushed past her, spun about to face her. He smiled and took her face tenderly in both hands, petting it.

"Sorry . . . you know I adore you, precious."

Then again he kissed her hard. She began to struggle and twist. She broke away. She stood off, panting.

"You be tender to me!" She babied out her mouth, pouting.

"All right, dearest."

He picked her up and carried her to the bed on his strong arms. He seated her on the edge and sat beside her, and kissed her shoulders softly. She felt his hands exploring. Then he had the zipper. He bared her upper body, lowering her gown gently. He began to kiss her breasts and upper body and to urge her back, until she lay flat. He lay kissing her, stroking her. Presently she lifted her arms around his back. She pressed her lips to his mouth and flicked the tip of her tongue against his.

She wanted him fiercely and immediately, but she fought against the rising wave of desire, recalling that he had gentled to her command. As she had wanted, as she had needed, and yet . . . what if, like John Barket, he quit if she struggled hard enough?

She pushed him away and sat up. She got to her feet. The gown was down to her hips. She stood writhing and stroking it down. It fell to the floor. She stepped out of it and stood off, arms uplifted, unpinning her hair.

She was wearing only black lace panties, very brief, cut in a high arc on the flare of her hip, and low in the center, exposing her navel and a few inches of enticingly curved lower belly. He sat watching her, enrapt, his mouth a little open. He stood up and began to take off his clothes, looking at her every minute.

"Nikki, I couldn't have dreamed you were this stunning."

"Did you dream?"

He shook his head several times. He took a long breath. "Taboo. You know you were absolutely taboo to me. I never let myself imagine you intimately. Never."

He moved to her again to touch her. He stroked her exposed body. He glided his right hand in under her panties to the rounds of her bottom. Then his left hand moved under the front. She sucked her breath sharply and went on tiptoes, the sensation of his touch setting her wild.

"Finish undressing," she whispered urgently. "I want to see you. I want to touch you!"

Then he was naked. She stripped off the lacy wisp covering her and stood naked for him. They gazed and touched each other. Then, impelled at the same moment, they went to the bed and lay wrapped in one another's arms, experiencing the simple animal pleasure of their nakedness against each other. She moved, rubbing her body to his.

He was well made, a good man. And his arousal was strong. He turned her easily into position on her back. His body moved within the embrace of her thighs. Then he was touching her intimately. The pleasure was so intense she began to throb. Fulfillment, she thought passionately, the fulfillment she had been yearning for her whole life. She wanted it . . . craved it . . . lusted feverishly for it.

But she pushed him violently. She began to cry and to protest.

"No! I don't want you. I'm afraid. No. No. *Stop!*"

She was rawly aware of what she was doing. It was cold and it was cruel, she castigated herself. But she must know if he could be turned back, if he *did* lack something. Nothing she could say or do now could reverse the truth of her fundamental being. Yes . . . If this could convince him it meant no, if his instinct was that faulty, she had to know. Her whole future was at stake.

He was poised, rigid, not moving forward or away. She renewed her protests. Intensified them. She began to give them full physical expression, twisting, kicking, trying to roll away, striking at him.

He looked at her dumbly, a kind of horror in his eyes. Then his mouth mashed shut. His hands caught her hips in a bruising grip. He held her as in a vise and thrust with all his force. He entered her deeply. She gasped with joy. Then he held her body and moved it forward and back, forward and back, without moving himself at all.

Unprotesting, she enjoyed it. She closed her eyes and began to smile voluptuously.

"Not so horrible?" he said in a half-rough, half-tender voice.

"I love it," she whispered. She lifted her arms and drew him down to cover her, to possess her totally.

When they had reached climax, they slept and woke and loved again. He woke her yet again in the night, and each time there was ecstasy.

The phone kept ringing all morning. Finally at eleven o'clock she answered. She lay listening, nodding, speaking briefly. She hung up and went back to sleep.

At one o'clock, Vic woke her.

"You're passionate *again?*" she giggled. "Then me, too!"

"Say, weren't you talking on the phone a few minutes ago?"

"A few hours ago." She glided her leg over his body with feline pleasure. She rolled with him and wrapped herself around him.

When they were done and had moved apart and Vic was smoking a cigarette, she said, "It was Anton calling."

"Oh? And . . . the reviews?"

He explained all about the power and non-power of the press. "While it's true that if the critics are unanimous, one way or the other, they can make or break a play, if the various critics disagree, they don't really affect the box office." She sighed.

"Well, we better get up and get the papers and read what they said. Mixed reviews, I take it."

"No. Unanimous." She rolled over onto her stomach and buried her face in the pillow. Her shoulders began to shake.

"Oh, Nikki, baby! I'm sorry. You poor kid. That's terrible! But you musn't cry, baby."

When he got her face turned and realized she was laughing, he swatted her naked bottom resoundingly, then began to laugh with her.

"Unanimously good!" She kicked her heels and bounced herself and laughed. "What could you have thought I meant? How could a play I choose to back turn out any other way? One would think that would be obvious. Just as it is that I make no mistake about a man. And you know why? I'll tell you why. It's simple. I'm wonderful!"

The End